Frederick Ross

Yorkshire Family Romance

Frederick Ross

Yorkshire Family Romance

ISBN/EAN: 9783337348625

Printed in Europe, USA, Canada, Australia, Japan

Cover: Foto ©Andreas Hilbeck / pixelio.de

More available books at **www.hansebooks.com**

FREDERICK ROSS, F.R.H.S.,

AUTHOR OF

"CELEBRITIES OF YORKSHIRE WOLDS," "PROGRESS OF CIVILISATION,"
ETC.

HULL:

WILLIAM ANDREWS & CO., THE .HULL PRESS.

LONDON: SIMPKIN, MARSHALL, HAMILTON, KENT, & CO.,
LIMITED.

———

1891.

Contents.

YORKSHIRE FAMILY ROMANCE.

The Synod of Streoneshalh.

NORTHUMBRIA was at peace, after a long period of anarchy, bloodshed, battles, and murders. Christianity had been restored by St. Oswald, King and Martyr; York Cathedral, commenced by King Eadwine, had been completed; the great Abbey of Lindisfarne had become a centre of Christian light and civilisation; and several other churches and religious houses were growing up over the length and breadth of the land. Oswy, a wise, vigorous, and warlike King, one of the most illustrious of his line, ruled Northumbria in its integrity; held northern Mercia under his sway; had subjected the southern Picts and Scots to his authority; and was Bretwalda of the Heptarchy. This position, however, he had only gained, and this peace firmly secured, after a

B

great struggle and the shedding of much blood, and, it must be added, after the perpetration of an atrocious crime. When Paulinus, under the patronage of King Eadwine, had introduced Christianity into Northumbria, Mercia was ruled by Penda, a ferocious Pagan, who made a vow to Woden that he would exterminate the new heretical faith or lay down his life in the attempt. Accordingly, he entered into a compact with Cadwallon, a British Prince of Wales, and together they invaded Northumbria. Eadwine met them in battle and was slain; Paulinus and the Queen, with her children, fled to Kent, and the kingdom was harried by the victors, who sought out the Christians and put them indiscriminately to the sword. Cadwallon remained as ruler of the kingdom, and under his barbarous measures Christianity became almost, if not altogether, extinct, whilst the altars of Woden were re-established in every direction. Osric and Eanfrid, grandsons of Ælla, first King of Deira, after the death of Eadwine, were raised by the voice of the people to the thrones of Deira and Bernicia. They had been baptised at the court of their uncle by Paulinus, but now, as they had no Christians to govern, they apostatised and relapsed into the faith of Woden, but their reign was short ; they laid siege to Cadwallon in York, were defeated, Osric slain in the battle, and Eanfrid put to death afterwards ; and Cadwallon continued to rule the Northumbrians with an iron hand.   At this time there was a young Prince, an exile in Scotland—Oswald, son of Æthelfred, King of Bernicia—who had fled thither when a youth, and had been instructed in the principles of Christianity by the monks of Iona.   He heard of the deaths of the two Kings, and of the misery to which his native land was subjected by the tyranny and oppression of Cadwallon, and determined upon going thither and attempting to drive out the usurper.   On his arrival the people flocked round his standard, and, with a cross borne in front of his army, he met Cadwallon at Deniseburn, near Hexham, and defeated him, Cadwallon falling in the fight.   He established his Court at York, as King of Northumbria, and eventually became Sixth Bretwalda, extending his territories beyond the Tweed.   He restored Christianity, by means of missionaries from Iona, completed the church of York, commenced by Eadwine, and founded other churches and some monasteries, leading a life of usefulness, beloved by his people for his piety and good government. But Penda was still living, as bitter as ever against Christianity, and intelligence reached the Court of York that he was preparing for a second invasion of Northumbria, again to trample out the nascent Christianity.   In order to be beforehand with his enemy, Oswald invaded Mercia, where the Pagan King was again victorious, and Oswald slain at Masserfield, which came, in consequence, to be called Oswald's-town, corrupted in modern times into Oswestry. Penda caused his body to be torn limb from limb and cast abroad to be devoured by wild beasts, then crossed the border into Northumbria, and ravaged the land with fire and sword.

When the Mercians had retired, Oswy, an illegitimate half-brother of Oswald, was called to the throne of Northumbria in the year 642 ; but two years afterwards, Oswin, son of Osric the Apostate, disputed his right on the ground of his illegitimacy, and being backed by a numerous body of friends, Oswy agreed to a compromise, he taking Bernicia, and Oswin Deira.   Seven years after, a dispute arose between the two Kings about the boundaries of their territories, and they took up arms to settle the question by the sword. The two armies met at Wulfer's Dun, near Catterick, when Oswin, perceiving the enemy's forces to be much more numerous than his own, and reluctant to shed blood recklessly, dismissed his men and went to the house of his friend Count Hudwold, at Ingethlin (Gilling), to conceal himself for the present, with a view of entering a monastery; but Hudwold betrayed him, and Oswy sent Ethelwin to murder him, who faithfully executed his mission. Eanfleda, Oswy's Queen, a daughter of King Eadwine, afterwards, with the consent of her husband, founded a monástery at Gilling, where prayers should be offered up for the soul of Oswin, and for the pardon of Oswy. The people of Deira refused to recognise Oswy as King; drove him back across the Tees when he came to take possession, and elected Æthelwald, a son of Oswald, for their King.

The hoary-headed old Pagan, Penda, although now well stricken in years, could not witness the advance of Christianity, under Oswy, without pious emotion, and he resolved upon still another invasion of Northumbria in the cause of Woden. He entered into an alliance with Athelm, King of the East Angles, and Æthelwald of Deira— the latter incited by motives of policy—and the confederates marched against Oswy.. A great battle ensued at Winwidfield, near Leeds, when Æthelwald, who was a Christian, repented of having entered into a league with the enemies of that faith, and stood aloof. After an obstinate fight, Penda and thirty of his chief officers were slain, and the greater part of his army cut to pieces. This was the last struggle in England between Christianity and Paganism.

Thus there was peace in the land after the scenes of violence and bloodshed occasioned by the fanatic fury of Penda, and Oswy found himself in a position to carry out his views for establishing Christianity on a sure basis. Before the ·battle of Winwidfield he had made a vow that he would build a great monastery at Streoneshalh, endow it with the twelve manors of Crown property lying round the White Bay (Whitby), and that he would dedicate his daughter Eanfleda to perpetual virginity and the service of God in the monastery, if he should, by the blessing of God, be successful over his Pagan enemy.

The Cathedral of York was now finished, and he sent the masons and other workmen to erect the monastery and church on the lofty cliff overhanging the outfall of the river Esk into the

White Bay, and its walls uprose with marvellous rapidity. As soon as it was completed it was opened for monks and nuns of the Benedictine order, a colony of whom migrated from Hartlepool; and the Princess Hilda, a woman highly esteemed for her learning, virtue, and piety, was placed at the head as Prioress. At this time there were two bodies of Christians in Northumbria, antagonistic to each other on many points of doctrine and ceremonial, the most important being the question of the proper time for the celebration of the Easter festival, and most important was it deemed in these primitive times, for both parties firmly believed that the soul's salvation was imperilled by its non-observance on the right day. The antagonistic sects were the priests and monks from Iona, representatives of the primitive British Church—which had been planted in the island, it was said, by Joseph of Arimathea—with their converts, comprehending the greater portion of the Northumbrian Christians; and on the other side, the ecclesiastics who had imbibed their faith at the feet of Romish teachers.

The origin of this antagonism of opinion came about in the following way. Christianity had been

extirpated in Northumbria by the sword of
Penda, and the people had relapsed into heathen-
ism, very few remaining who still clung to the
faith as taught by Paulinus. This was the state
of the country when Oswald came to the throne.
He had imbibed the tenets of Christianity in the
schools of Iona, and sent thither for missionaries
to re-convert his people, and founded the see of
Lindisfarne, which became the focus of religion
and civilisation in his kingdom. Thus, when
Oswy ascended the throne, Christianity of the
ancient British type prevailed in the land. But
there were others who had been educated in
Southern England, France, and Italy, who held
to the faith as promulgated by Augustine,
Paulinus, and other Roman missionaries, and a
great deal of controversy, disputation, and even
quarrels on tenets of belief and religious obser-
vances, took place between the two divisions of the
Church. First and foremost, as stated above, was
that of the proper time for observing the festival
of Easter. The British Church celebrated it on
the day of the full moon next after the vernal
equinox; the Romish, not on the day of the full
moon, but on the Sunday following. The former
claimed St. John, the beloved apostle, and the

usage of the Eastern Church, as their authorities; the latter, the example of Saints Peter and Paul, backed by a decree of the council of Nice, and they branded as schismatics all who refused to conform to their mode; whilst the British condemned to hell-fire all who deferred the celebration until the Sunday after the full moon. Bede said "It was not without reason that the question disturbed the minds of a great number of Christians, who were apprehensive lest after they had begun the race of salvation they should be found to have run in vain." This state of things caused great confusion, one section of the Church humbling themselves in abstinence, prayers, and tears, whilst the other were lifting up their voices in joyful celebration of the Resurrection. Even in the King's Palace there was disunion, Oswy, who had been educated in Scotland, and Eanfleda, his Queen, who had been taught in Kent, observing the festival, one on the one day, the other on the other.

It was obvious that something must be done to put an end to these disputes, and Oswy at length determined upon calling together a Synod to settle the matter once and for all. There was also another question on which the two sections of

the Church were at daggers drawn, that of the
tonsure, the Romish monks shaving the head
all round, emblematic of the crown of thorns;
the British only in front as far back as the
ears; but this was not looked upon as a vital
question, and was easily arranged after the great
Easter dispute was settled.

The King decided upon holding the Synod in
his new monastery of Streoneshalh, and had
summoned all the most notable ecclesiastics on
both sides to discuss the question. It was a
picturesque spectacle to see the Royal train and
the monks and priests winding their way up the
steep hill from the valley of the Esk and entering
the portals of the priory on the summit, where it
stood overlooking the expanse of sea, with its
rounded arches and stunted pillars, radiant in
the sunshine, and glitteringly white in the
freshness of its architecture. The disputants
assembled in the great hall, the King taking his
place on the dais as president, with the prioress
Hilda by his side.

On the Scottish side were ranged Hilda, who,
although she had been baptised by Paulinus,
had been instructed at the feet of Aidan, the
Ionian Bishop of Lindisfarne; Colman, Bishop of

Lindisfarne ; Cedd (a Northumbrian), Bishop of the East Saxons ; and a train of monks and priests from Icolmkill and Lindisfarne. On the Romish side were Queen Eanfleda ; Prince Alfred, son of Oswy ; Wilfrid, Abbot of Ripon, who had been educated in Rome, a most able, eloquent, and learned man, the first Churchman of his age ; Agilbert, Bishop of Paris, formerly of the West Saxons ; James, the deacon who had been left by Paulinus in charge of the infant Northumbrian Church ; Ronan and Agathon, priests who had been educated in France, and others who had received instruction from Italian priests and monks.

Oswy maintained a neutrality as president, although he adhered to the British mode ; and Cedd acted as interpreter.

The King opened the Synod by briefly stating its object, the necessity of conformity in so important a point as that it was called together to discuss, praying the Holy Spirit to guide them in the debate ; and concluded by calling upon Bishop Colman to open the discussion.

The Bishop said that Easter, as observed by his Church, was derived directly from the Apostles, not from a Romish bishop or a council of fallible men. Bishops Finan, Aidan, and Columba had so observed it; but their authority, though eminently holy men, was not sufficient. Their warrant was based on the custom of St. John, the beloved disciple of Christ, therefore, recognising his high authority, and the fact that it was so observed by the Eastern and eldest-born Church, no one could dispute its being the true method.

Bishop Agilbert was called upon to reply, but excused himself, as not knowing the Northumbrian tongue sufficiently well to make himself understood. Wilfrid, the Abbot, the great champion of his side, whose name was afterwards known from Rome to York, and who became Archbishop of York, thereupon rose and said, " Easter, as we observe it, is the same as we ourselves have seen it observed at Rome, where the blessed apostles, Saint Peter and Paul, lived, preached, suffered, and are buried; and as, in our travels through Italy and France, whether for study or pilgrimage, we have always seen it observed. We know also, by relation, that the same obtains in the Churches of Asia, Africa, Egypt, and Greece, nay, among all the churches of the world, excepting in this remote and obscure island, where a few obstinate Britons pretend to dispute the affair with the whole world."

At this taunt Bishop Colman said, " I marvel, brother Wilfrid, that you call ours a foolish contention, when we have for our pattern and guide so worthy an apostle as St. John, who alone leaned upon our Saviour's breast."

Wilfrid, touched with compunction at having spoken too harshly, replied, " God forbid that I should accuse St. John," and entered into a learned statement of the early Christians accommodating their rites and ceremonies in accordance with those of the Jews, and that St. John, who kept the laws of Moses literally, thus celebrated the feast of Easter on the first day of the Jewish Passover, whether on Sunday or any other day. But St. Peter, knowing that Christ rose from the grave on a Sunday, celebrated the feast on that day of the week, in accordance with a command which he received from our Lord, which is certainly a higher authority than that of St. John; and the decree of the council of Nice, in 525, was but a confirmation thereof. Colman replied, " Athanolius, so commendable for his holiness, and Father Columba, whose

sanctity is proved by miracles, kept Easter as we
do, and I do not deem it wise to depart from
their method."

"Their holiness and miracles," responded
Wilfrid, "I dispute not; but I have no doubt
that when, in the day of judgment, they say,
'Lord, have we not prophesied, cast out devils, and
wrought miracles in Thy name?' He will answer,
'Begone; I know you not.' Can you compare
Columba with the most blessed of the Apostles, to
whom Christ said, 'Thou art Peter, and upon
this rock I will build my church, and the gates of
hell shall not prevail against it; and to thee I
give the keys of the kingdom of heaven.'"

"Did our Lord speak this to St. Peter?"
asked the King, of Colman.

"Most certainly," was the reply.

"Hitherto," continued the King, "I have
observed the rule of St. John, and in ignorance,
but now mine eyes are opened. You both agree
that the words of our Lord, quoted by the Father
Abbot, were spoken to St. Peter, and I deem it
not wise to withstand or gainsay so potent a
person as the doorkeeper of heaven, lest when I
come thither I find them closed against me; and
I should recommend this assembly to decide

upon celebrating the festival after the mode of St. Peter." The result of this speech was that several went over from the British to the Roman side, and, after a few other speeches, the question was put to the vote, and decided almost unanimously in favour of the Romanists. Cedd, Bishop of the East Saxons, was one of the converts, but Colman declined submission, soon after resigned his bishopric, and with his monks and priests returned to Iona.

Ultimately, however, all the branches of the Church conformed to the rule of St. Peter—the Picts in 699, the Scots, comprehending the monks of Iona, in 716, and the Britons or Welsh in 800.

The Doomed Heir of Osmotherley.

HE Vale of Mowbray is one of the many beautiful pieces of landscape scenery with which the county of Yorkshire abounds; a favourite sketching-ground for artists, and often seen, in detached portions, on the walls of the Royal Academy. An equal favourite, also, is it with the tourist and worshippers of natural beauty. If Dr. Syntax, when he mounted Grizzle to go in search of the picturesque, had come to the Vale of Mowbray, we may fancy that he would have considered his quest at an end, and his purpose accomplished.

In the Saxon era it presented a somewhat different aspect from what it does now; more strikingly magnificent and grand in its wild, natural beauty. Instead of cornfields, pastures, hedgerows, churches, mills, and mansions, it was one expanse of forest, with towering oaks, elms, and poplars; and, beneath a tangled undergrowth of brushwood and briar, the home and haunts of the antlered stag, the wild boar, the wolf, and innumerable other wild creatures, four-footed, on the sward below, or pinion-borne amid the foliage above. It must not be supposed, however, that the vale was given up entirely to these denizens of woodland, and destitute of human inhabitants. The Lord of the valley was Earl Oswald, a Saxon, or, to speak more accurately, an Anglian nobleman—the greatest landed proprietor for many miles round. His mansion was seated on a gentle slope of the Hambleton Hills; a one-storied edifice, consisting of a large hall, where he, his retainers, and domestic servants, partook of their meals, and where the latter slept by night, on straw or rushes spread on the floor, with some smaller family sleeping and guest rooms, a kitchen, brewhouse, and other necessary appliances of a nobleman's household, including a chapel with open, round-headed doorway, draped with a pair of woollen portieres, generally looped back, and displaying in the interior some roughly carpentered benches, and a lamp pendant from the roof.

Around the mansion was some arable land, with granaries and stacks; pasture land for horses, oxen, and sheep, protected by stockades

c

from the incursions of wolves and other beasts
of prey; an orchard and a vegetable garden.
Scattered about in clearings of the forest were
the homesteads of the class correspondent with
the modern tenant-farmer, with their oxen,
swine, wains, and rude implements of husbandry;
and, nestling around the mansion, an aggregation
of wattled and mud-built dwellings, the abodes
of the villeins or serfs, hence denominated a village,
in the centre of which stood the church, a very
primitive structure of wood, consisting of nave
and chancel only, without side aisles, transept, or
tower.

Earl Oswald was a young man of five-and-
twenty years, comely in aspect and benign in
manner; and was a considerate overlord and
kind master. He had not long been in possession of his estates, his father having died only
twelve months previously, his death having been
occasioned by an accident when pursuing the
wild boar in .the forest. The present Earl was
the last of his race, having no brothers or other
relatives to inherit the earldom, which would
become extinct in case of his death without
issue; consequently it behoved him, in order to
continue the succession, to look out for a wife.

But at that time the choice was very limited; it was essential that he should marry a lady with some pretensions to aristocratic birth, in order to keep up the dignity of his family; and as people, even nobles, did not then travel far away from home, visiting only such families as resided within a moderate distance, his choice was rather restricted. It happened, however, that one day, when hunting in Cleveland, he met with a Thegn, one of the lower order of nobility, who invited him to his house to spend the night, as he was some distance from home. At supper he was introduced to the Thegn's daughter, Gytha, a beautiful young maiden, some three or four years younger than himself, and was so charmed with her beauty, amiability of deportment, and sensible conversation, that he became enamoured of her, and mentally resolved that if there were no obstacles in the way he would make her his countess and the mother of his heir. He made no declaration on that occasion, but finding the hunting round the bases of the great Cleveland hill, the Ottenberg, now called Roseberry Topping, fruitful of sport, he came again and again, seldom letting a week pass without one or two visits, and never failing to call at the

Thegn's house, where he was always cordially
welcomed by Gytha and her father.   The friend-
ship thus commenced' soon ripened into intimacy,
and when the Earl found that his attentions had
made an impression on the heart of the fair
maiden, he began to whisper in her ear the
tale of love.   As maidens, in those practical,
unsophisticated days, knew not the art of
coquetry, and were not apt at disguising the
feelings of their hearts, Gytha listened with
pleasure to his flattering tale, confessed at once
that she reciprocated his love, and without any
needless circumlocution or affected bashfulness consented to become his wife, which met with the full
approbation of her father, and a month afterwards he bore her away to become the mistress
of the mansion in the Mowbray Vale, and, it was
hoped, the mother of the future lord of the
domain.

Months past along—delicious months—one
succession of honeymoons; the happy pair never
tiring of each other's company.   In the mornings
the Earl would go forth to superintend the
operations of ploughing, sowing, or harvesting, or
to look after the careful tending of his flocks and
herds; and occasionally, for pastime or for the

benefit of the larder, would penetrate the recesses of the forest, hunting-spear in hand, and surrounded by his hounds; whilst the Lady Gytha directed the domestic affairs of the house, or occupied herself in her bower, with her handmaidens, embroidering a set of arras for the adornment of the hall; but they always spent the after-part of the day together in caressing converse.

The months thus passed along, and began to resolve themselves into years, but still the great hope of their lives was not accomplished, that of giving an heir to carry downwards the honours and possessions of the family. For a long time they flattered themselves with this hope, despite the length of time that had elapsed since their marriage; but when three or four years had gone into the past without any fruition of their hopes, they began to despond. The Earl became moody and melancholy in contemplating the probable and almost certain extinction of his race; and his lady wept and mourned in secret, at the bitter disappointment her husband experienced, no less than at the denial to herself of the delights and pleasant anxieties of maternity.

Another year or two, with their wintry storms

and summer sunshine, went by, and the Earl had
sunk into the depths of despair, when, after all
hope had departed, a gleam of sunshine shot
athwart "the winter of his discontent," heralding
the coming of a glorious summer. The probable
birth of a living child, and, it might be, heir, was
announced to him, and he immediately became a
changed man ; from the slough of despondency
he sprang up, radiant with expectancy, buoyant
in spirit, and gladdened at heart; and the Lady
Gytha underwent an equal change, from tears
and brooding to the delicious anticipation of
fondling on her breast and presenting to her
husband, as the outcome of their loves, an heir
to his lands and dignities.

It was a proud day for Earl Oswald when the
women of his household brought him news of the
birth of a male child, healthy and well-formed,
with promise of developing into vigorous life,
indeed, in the nurse's opinion, it was one of the
most wonderful infants that ever came into the
world, and he was further gratified to learn that
the mother was doing well, whom he waited
upon as soon as the feminine portion of the
community, who ruled supreme at this interesting
crisis, permitted, to congratulate her on the

auspicious event. Nor did he confine himself to
mere gratulations and expressions of rejoicing;
in demonstration of his gratitude to Heaven for
his long-hoped-for heir, every day, for the succeed-
ing week, he sat at the entrance door of his
mansion and administered, with bountiful hand,
food and stycas to all mendicant wayfarers,
dispensed gifts to his servitors and slaves, and
bestowed liberal donations on the Church and
the monastic fraternities, with a stipulation in
the latter case that they should pray for the
welfare of the newly-born Christian child.

The infant throve apace, and waxed more
beautiful every day, with his blue Saxon eyes
and fair flaxen hair, the darling of his mother,
the cherished hope of his father, and the petted
plaything of all the household. He had attained
the mature age of twelve months, when a
terrible calamity befel the family, a calamity,
however, which was common enough in those
days of turbulence, bloodshed, and war. It was
the time when the Danish Vikings were most
active in making landings on the British coasts,
ravaging the country, and massacring the people
who opposed them, and then sailing homeward
with the spoils of the plundered villages and

monasteries. Northumbria lay especially open
to their incursions; Ravenspurn, Flamborough,
and Lindisfarne, were their principal landing
places, and the Humber, the Tees, and the Tyne,
their high roads into the interior. They had,
indeed, established a permanent encampment on
the headland of Flamborough, and intrenched
themselves by enlarging a natural ravine,
deepening it, and throwing up earthworks, so as
to constitute it a formidable defensive barrier
stretching across the peninsula, which still exists,
and is popularly known as "Danes' Dyke."

News reached Earl Oswald that a large fleet of
vessels had arrived at Flamborough, and that the
Danes, in great numbers, were marching with
sword and firebrand across the Wolds, and in the
direction of his home. The news was sent by
the leading men of the district, who were
gathering their vassals and slaves together to
resist the invaders, and he was requested to come
to their assistance with all the men he could
muster. He lost no time in obeying the call,
and after bidding an affectionate farewell to his
wife, and exhorting her to great watchfulness and
care over little Oswy, who, said he, is the only
hope for the continuance of my race in case of

any mischance to myself—he went forth at the head of his retainers, and joined the army, which had assembled in the neighbourhood of Driffield, to check the progress of the enemy.

About a couple of miles to the north-east of Driffield, there was a valley running east and west, along which it was anticipated the foe would come, and here the Saxons decided to await their approach. They took up their position on the southern slopes, and threw up some rough earthworks to protect their front, and, after lying there a couple of days, their scouts brought intelligence that the Danes were but a mile distant, and that in their track could be seen the flames of villages which they had fired in their march. Presently they made their appearance; a vast host of fierce-looking warriors, who, on perceiving the Saxons, set up a wild barbarian shout, and clashed their weapons together as if eager for the conflict. The Saxons uttered a shout of defiance in response, but remained quietly behind their intrenchments, whilst the Danes rushed forward impetuously, and clambering up the slope, the battle began. The field was obstinately contested on both sides, the fight lasting the entire day, neither gaining any absolute advantage, the bravery being equal on both sides, and what the Saxons lacked in numbers was made up by the superiority of their position, and the shelter afforded by their earthworks. Great numbers of brave men fell on both sides, the Danes, from their exposed position, losing more than their antagonists, and when the darkness of night fell, separating the combatants, they deemed it expedient to retreat upon Flamborough.

The following day the Saxons went over the field to succour the wounded and bury the dead. Among the former was found Earl Oswald, who was taken in charge by his retainers and conveyed to his home; and the latter were buried, Saxon and Dane together, and tumuli raised over their bodies. Their grave-mounds may still be seen spread over two or three acres of ground, over-canopied by trees, and are popularly known by the name of " Danes' Graves," and the valley where the battle was fought still bears the name of " Danes' Dale."

A speedy messenger was sent to inform Lady Gytha of what had befallen her husband, and it was with anguished heart that she received the mournful cavalcade which carried him, wounded and almost insensible, to his home. He lived two or three days, but in the end, despite the most skilful of leechery and the most assiduous nursing, he succumbed to the loss of blood he had sustained during the night he lay on the field. In his dying moments he again besought his wife to protect and bring up in godly fashion his infant heir; and she, with heartbroken sobbing, entreated him to have no apprehensions on that head, as now she would have nothing to live for but that one sole purpose. And the Earl closed his eyes in death, and was buried in the little wooden church hard by, which had been built by his grandfather—buried with all the pomp befitting his rank; and the Lady Gytha returned to her mansion to grieve over her loss, devote herself to the instruction of her beloved child, and look after the interests of his estates.

It chanced one day that the widowed lady and her orphan child were disporting themselves on the grass-plot in front of the house, when a withered old crone came up and implored charity. The Lady Gytha, who was ever beneficent to the poor, sent into the house for some victuals, which she gave to the old woman, bidding her sit under the shade of a tree and eat thereof, condoled with her under her infirmities, and supplemented her gift of food with a few coins. Whilst she was conversing with the woman, the little Oswy was running about after some ducks, and, chasing them to the edge of a pond, fell in, but was immediately rescued. At the same moment a dog that was chained up near by gave two prolonged howls, which attracted the attention of the stranger, who, after musing awhile, said, " Lady ! you have been very kind in your largesses to me, whom you know not, and I can only repay you by a warning, which I pray you to take heed of. I am an old woman, and have lived long in this world, not without learning somewhat that is hidden to others. I have studied omens and forebodings, and have acquired the power of predicting the future from signs of the present. Know then, lady, that I can foresee from the mishap of your little son, and the language of the dog, that he will undergo great peril from water, and that this will happen, unless prevented by fit precaution, in his second year, as is indicated by the two howls of the dog ; " and, having said this, she hobbled off, leaning on her walking-staff, without leaving time for reply.

Lady Gytha, although she did not place much credence in the prediction of the old woman, was imbued, to some extent, with the superstitions and credulities of the age, and she summoned into her presence an astrologer, requesting him to cast the nativity of the child. He noted down the time and particulars of his birth, and promised a reply within the week. After a few days' absence he returned, and appeared before Lady Gytha with a clouded brow, she receiving him with a tremor of anxiety. "What do the stars reveal?" enquired she. "Are the tidings good or evil?" "Lady," replied he, "I have calculated the star of his nativity, and sorry am I to tell that it augurs evil rather than good. A great peril awaits the child, on the fourth day of the third moon after his second birthday. It is recorded in the starry volume that on that occasion he will perish by drowning."

"Oh, say not so, wise sir. It would kill me as well. Are you assured that this fate is inevitable?"

" Fate, lady, is inevitable; but there is one planet which presents a disturbing element in his horoscope, and it is possible that this fate may have been miscalculated, and that, through the

influence of the planet, the threatening may be
averted; and it will become you that, at the
date indicated, you should take all possible precaution, in order that he should not be brought
into the neighbourhood of water of any kind."

The astrologer, having been rewarded gene-
rously for his services, and assured that all due
precautions should be taken, he departed,
murmuring to himself, "Fate is fate, and it
cannot be averted."

The Lady Gytha's whole existence was now
absorbed in that of her child. He was scarcely
ever out of her reach and sight, she watched over
him with more than maternal care, if that were
possible, and he continued to blossom out, with
the promise of becoming everything she could wish
—her support, her comfort, and the pride of her
after-life. But these prospects of the future were
overshadowed by a cloud—an anxious foreboding
of what might happen on the fourth day of the
third moon of his second year, which the stars
marked with a doubtful and perhaps fatal prog-
nostic. Could he but pass that dangerous point
of life, the lowering cloud would dissolve into
thin air, and for the future might be anticipated
the glad sunshine of existence.

The fatal day came nearer and nearer. He
had passed his second birthday, and the mother
had meditated often and often on the means
whereby he should be delivered from the threatening evil. It was plainly revealed to her that
the danger arose from water, and she reasoned
that if she could place him out of the neighbourhood of river, pools, or springs, the evil might be
turned aside and the augury baffled. When
thinking the matter over, there suddenly rose up
before her mind's eye the steep slopes of Ottenberg, the Cleveland hill, about which she had
often clambered and gambolled when a child,
and it struck her that if she could convey young
Oswy to the summit, he would be removed so far
away from any running or standing stream, or
pool of water, that there could be no possibility
of the fulfilment of the prediction, and she
resolved upon taking him thither.

Accordingly she proceeded to her father's
house at its base, and on the summer's night
preceding the fateful day, clomb the side of the
hill with her child in her arms. She arrived at
the summit as the sun was rising from the sea
on the eastern horizon, and lighting up the
glorious panorama visible from that elevated

position. She partook of some refreshment which she had brought with her, and, although she felt no fatigue in making the ascent, owing to her anxiety, now that she had reached what she deemed a place of security, nature began to give way, and a sense of exhaustion to oppress her. She sat there, with her child clasped in her arms, as the sun rose higher in the heavens, and darted forth its heated rays upon her unsheltered head. Under its influence she began to feel drowsy, but battled with the feeling, determined not to lose her hold of the child until the day had passed. At length, however, she unconsciously and insensibly succumbed, and fell asleep, sinking on the turf and relaxing her grasp. The young Oswy disengaged himself, and wandered away, plucking the wild flowers, and looking with infant delight at the gulls winging their flight over the sea.

An hour or two elapsed, and the Lady Gytha awoke. At first she could scarcely understand where she was, but in a few minutes she came to full consciousness, and was startled to find that her child was not with her. She sprang up, called him by name, but elicited no response, and she feared he had fallen down the side of the hill. With beating heart she sought around, and on turning a projecting shoulder of the hill was agonised to perceive the object of her search lying with his face in a stream of water that was issuing from a fissure, and, on taking him up, found life to be extinct. The pen fails in attempting to depict her frantic grief, but it may be briefly stated, that she carried down the lifeless body, conveyed it to her home, and laid it beside its father in the little timber church. For her there was no further earthly joy, and fixing her thoughts on the only source of consolation, she founded a small religious house in the Vale of Mowbray, where she spent the few remaining years of her life in religious meditation and devotional exercises. She was buried beside her beloved child in the little church, around which a village grew up, which was called, in remembrance of the burial-place of Oswy and his mother—Osmotherley.

According to the legend, the spring at the summit of the hill gushed forth miraculously, in order that the decree of Fate should not be frustrated.

" On the proud steep of Ottenberg still may be found
  The spring which rose his sad doom to complete;
And on its verge the villagers sit round,
  In wonder recording the fiat of Fate."

Eadwine, the Royal Martyr.

 PIOUS and benevolent monk of Rome, passing one day through the slave market of that city, noticed a group of beautiful fair-haired boys and youths, who were exposed for sale. Compassionating their condition, he enquired whence they came. "They are Angles," was the reply. "They are beautiful enough to be *angeli*," said the monk. "What part of Anglia come they from?" "Deira." "Then shall they be saved, *de ira*, from the wrath of God. Who is their King?" "Ælla." "Then," continued the monk, "shall Alleluias resound through their land," and he there and then determined to go thither as a missionary, and preach the Gospel to them, but before he could could complete his arrangements, he was raised to the Pontifical throne as Gregory I., afterwards called Gregory the Great. Incapable, therefore, of going himself, he sent Augustine, with Paulinus and other monks, as

missionaries to the Saxons of Britain. Instead, however, of going to the kingdom of Deira, they landed in that of Kent, gained the ear of King Ethelberht, who embraced Christianity, and established the see of Canterbury, with Augustine as Bishop thereof.

Ælla, the first king of Deira, died in the year 588, leaving a son, his heir, then three years of age, and an elder daughter, Acca, married to Ethelfrid, King of Bernicia, the great kingdom of Northumbria being then divided into Bernicia and Deira, both extending from sea to sea, and separated by the river Tees. Taking advantage of his brother-in-law's tender age, Ethelfrid usurped the throne of Deira, and became King of the whole of Northumbria, and the boy Eadwine was taken into exile by his friends. For many years, until he grew up to manhood, he wandered about from one refuge to another, until at last he found a safe asylum at the court of Redwald, King of the East Angles. Ethelfrid sent a demand that he should be delivered up to him, and Redwald, in reply, said to the messenger, "Tell thy master that I have promised to protect him, and will not give him up at the dictate of any King, however powerful he may be." Eventually, however, persuaded by bribes, and terrified by threats, he agreed to deliver him up. Eadwine, hearing of this, wandered forth into the forest, and, " as he sate solitary under a tree, in dumps, musing what was best to be done," a venerable stranger suddenly appeared before him, and said, "Noble Prince, thou knowest me not, but I come to tell thee that thou shalt be restored to thy kingdom, and moreover shall become Bretwalda of the Saxon Kings, if thou listenest but to those that shall be sent to thee, to teach the worship of the only true God." Eadwine, dazzled by the prospect, readily promised to do so, when the stranger placed his hand upon his head, saying, "Remember that as a sign," and vanished as mysteriously as he had appeared. On his return to the palace, he found that, at the intercession of the Queen, Redwald had withdrawn from his engagement, and was now determined to protect the fugitive to the utmost of his power. Ethelfrid, in consequence, raised an army for the invasion of East Anglia, but was met by Redwald, and a desperate battle ensued on the banks of the river Idle, in which the usurper was defeated and slain, and Eadwine proclaimed King of Northumbria. He proved himself to be an able and vigorous ruler, adding the Isles of Man and Anglesea to his dominions, and extending his territories northward to the Forth, where he built a fortress, around which a town gradually grew up, which was called Edwin's burgh—the infant Edinburgh. He raised his kingdom to a height of power it had never before attained, and in the year 624, on the death of Redwald, he attained the dignity of Bretwalda, or Supreme King of the Saxons, and President of the Heptarchian Witenagemot, whenever any such should be called together.

His first wife, Quenborga, daughter of Ceorl, King of Mercia, having died, he sent Ambassadors to ask the hand of Ethelburga, daughter of Ethelberht, King of Kent, in marriage, but her brother, Eadberht, then on the throne, replied, " I cannot consent, for it is not meet that a Christian Princess should mate with a pagan." The Ambassadors returned to Northumbria, and extolled so highly the beauty and amiability of the Princess, that Eadwine determined to make her his Queen at any cost, and, after some further negotiation, agreed that she should enjoy her own religion, have priests to celebrate the rites thereof, and, moreover, that he would himself examine the grounds of the Christian faith, and if he found them superior to those of Woden, would renounce the latter and embrace the former. Accordingly the fair young Christian came to Northumbria, accompanied by Paulinus and three or four preaching monks, and the marriage was celebrated with great splendour at York, the Pope sending her, on the occasion, a silver mirror and a gilt ivory comb, which latter is supposed to have been found near Whitby in 1872.

Faithful to his stipulation, the King allowed his Queen the utmost freedom in religious matters, and permitted the monks to go forth throughout his realm, preaching and making proselytes. Still he himself adhered to the worship of Woden, in the great temple of Goodmandingham, over which Coifi presided as high priest, and which was contiguous to one of his palaces—that of Londesborough, near Market Weighton. About this time Cuichelm, King of Wessex, jealous of his ascendancy as Bretwalda, sent a messenger to assassinate him, who failed in his object, and Eadwine prepared to make war against Cuichelm for his dastardly conduct. Two days after this event his daughter Eanfleda was born, and, at the urgent request of the Queen and Paulinus, he permitted her to be baptised and dedicated to the service of the God of his Queen, as a thank-offering for his escape. He promised Paulinus also, that if his God were sufficiently potent to give him a victory over Cuichelm, he would, on his return, take into serious consideration the question of embracing Christianity and proclaiming it the religion of Northumbria. At the close of their conversation, Paulinus placed his hand on the King's head, and said, " You have been restored to your kingdom, you have extended its limits, and become the greatest of the Saxon kings of England—the Bretwalda—know you this sign ? " Eadwine replied that he did. "And," continued Paulinus, " there was another promise besides these of a secular nature, that teachers should be sent to instruct you in the true faith. Behold, here we are—I and my companions." This was more convincing to the King than any amount of logical argument, and he marched with confidence into Wessex, gained a decisive victory, and on his return summoned a gemôt of nobles at his Londesborough Palace to discuss this great religious question.

The chief speaker at the assembly was the high priest Coifi. "Know, O King!" said he, "that I have long been of opinion that our gods are worthless, and can do nothing for us, and I now perceive that the God of Paulinus is God alone, the creator of the world, and the true object of worship." The King acquiesced in his views, and the nobles, taking their cue from them, gave their assent to the deposition of Woden, and the substitution of Christ as the God of the Saxons.

It was then determined that the great temple of Woden should be desecrated, and the King inquired who would dare to do it. "I," replied Coifi, "I have spent my life hitherto in ministering at the altar of a false and impotent god, and it is fitting that I should overturn that altar." A day was fixed for the purpose, and then the King and his nobles, followed by a crowd of people, proceeded from Londesborough to Goodmandingham, and in the midst Coifi, mounted on a war steed and brandishing a lance in his hand. As the priests of Woden were only permitted to ride mares, and not to bear arms of any kind, the people gazed upon him with superstitious horror, expecting that either the

earth would open and swallow him, or a thunderbolt descend from the sky and strike him dead ; but
neither occurred, and the sun shone as serenely as
if no such monstrous act of impiety were taking
place. Without hesitation Coifi rode boldly
into the temple, and, poising his lance, hurled it
at the idol, upon which the people without, not
daring to enter, fearing lest the temple should
fall and bury them in its ruins, set up a loud
yell of horror, and flung themselves down on the
sward, but when they beheld the lance quivering
in the side of the image and the priest calmly
riding out, without the slightest manifestation of
wrath on the part of the outraged god—neither
thunder, lightning, nor earthquake—they began
to think that Woden was no god, and that he
whom Paulinus proclaimed was a God indeed,
and the issue was that the King and his Court
were baptised, and then the common people,
10,000 having undergone the rite in the river
Swale in one day, going into the river in batches,
whilst Paulinus blessed the water. A wooden
church was erected in York, which was replaced
by one of stone, commenced by Eadwine and
completed by King Oswald—the precursor of the
present majestic York Minster, and Paulinus

was constituted Bishop of the See, which comprehended the whole of England northward of the Humber and the Mersey. In 634, Pope Honorius sent him a pallium, which raised him to the dignity of an Archbishop.

At that time the kingdom of Mercia was ruled by a ferocious old pagan—Penda—who made a vow to extirpate Christianity from the island, and entered into an alliance with Cadwallon, a Welsh King, for the invasion of Northumbria. Eadwine encountered them at Heathfield, near Doncaster, and a sanguinary battle ensued, which proved most disastrous to the hitherto victorious Northumbrians. Eadwine and his son Osfrid were slain in the fight, and another son, Eanfrid, was murdered after the battle. The victors then ravaged the country, burning and plundering the houses, and slaughtering the people without regard to sex or age. Cadwallon remained in Northumbria, assuming the government, and ruling the people with great severity and cruelty, until he was slain in battle by Oswald, whilst Penda marched into East Anglia, which had become Christian, subdued it, and then took upon himself the title of Bretwalda. Thus fell the great and glorious Eadwine, the victor of many fights, the Bretwalda of England, the first Christian King of the North, and the proto-martyr of Northumbria. His body was conveyed to Whitby for burial, and his head interred in the porch of his church at York. He was after-wards canonised, and a church in London and another at Breve, in Somersetshire, have been dedicated to St. Eadwine. The Queen, with her two surviving children, accompanied by Paulinus, fled to Kent. She founded a nunnery, and took the veil within its walls; her children she sent to France, to be educated under the care of her cousin, King Dagobert, and after her death she was canonised. Paulinus became the third Bishop of Rochester.

Siward, the Viceroy.

ACCORDING to a Scandinavian legend, a young Danish lady went wandering into a forest, where she suddenly, when turning out of one glade into another, came face to face with a bear, who seized her and forcibly violated her. The result was the birth of a child, with shaggy ears, to whom was given the name of Barn. He married, and had a son, Siward, who came on a piratical excursion to England, and became Viceroy Earl of Northumbria, and this identity of Siward, son of Barn, with Siward the Earl, has been generally accepted by modern chroniclers, which may be attributed to the great obscurity which hangs over the history of this period. The fact is, that this legend does not pertain to Earl Siward at all, but to another Siward—Siward-Barn—who lived half-a-century afterwards, and was son of the Danish Jarl—Barn. Following the instincts of his race, he sailed from Denmark with a fleet, and after ravaging the Orkneys and the coasts of Scotland and Northumbria, passed up the Thames, and presented himself at the Court of Edward the Confessor, whose favour he gained by entering his service. He was rewarded with lands in Cumberland and Westmoreland, and in Holderness, Yorkshire, one of his manors there being called Barns-town, now Barmston, near Bridlington. After the conquest, he joined in the northern insurrection against William I., and was one of the companions of Hereward the Wake in the Isle of Ely, where he was captured, sent a prisoner into Normandy, and there died. He never had anything to do with the Earldom of Northumbria, which was held during his time by Tosti, Morkere, and Waltheof, the son of Earl Siward.

Having disposed of this myth, it becomes us to give, as far as can be ascertained, the true ancestry of Siward. When the Saxon heptarchy, or octarchy, became consolidated into one kingdom, the realm of Northumbria, extending from the Humber to the Tweed, and sometimes to the Forth, which was the last to submit, was peopled by a brave and warlike people, sensitively tenacious of their independence, and of so

turbulent a character, that it became necessary
to place over them a Viceroy Earl of great
vigour, determination, and military ability, to
give it the semblance of semi-independence, but
at the same time to be ready on the spot to nip
incipient rebellion when in the bud. Such a
Governor was found in Oswulf, son of Ealdred,
Lord of Bamborough, who was nominated to the
office by King Athelstane. He was succeeded
by Waltheof, the Elder, who was followed by his
son Ughtred, from whom the holders of not less
than seven peerages claim descent. By Ælgifu,
daughter of King Ethelred II., he had issue—
Eadulf, Gospatric, and Ældred. Ældred succeeded as Earl of Bernicia, on the death of his
uncle, Eadulf I., Earl of Northumbria; and
Siward, who was his son, appears to have been
appointed, at the same time, Deputy-Earl of
Deira.

He was born towards the end of the tenth
century, was a giant in stature, of Herculean
strength, and of great courage, which he displayed on many a field of battle. His life, indeed,
appears to have been spent more in the battlefield than in the peaceful pursuits of government,
the administration of justice, or the superintendence

of his Yorkshire manors, of which Malton was the chief, granted to him for his military services, and it presents a succession of romantic episodes, in which the sword played the principal part.

Ældred, his father, died in 1038, and was succeeded in Bernicia by his brother, Eadulf II. Siward, however, claimed it as his hereditary right; and so matters remained until 1041, when Eadulf incurred the displeasure of King Hathacnut. This was the opportunity Siward had been longing for, and he hastened up to the King's Court, where, by his representations, he embittered the mind of the King still further against his uncle, and in the sequel was either ordered or permitted to put him to death. This was precisely what he wanted, and, without the least scruple of conscience or regard to kinship when his own aggrandisement was at issue, he proceeded to Bernicia and murdered his uncle in cold blood, assuming at the same time the government, and thus becoming Earl of Northumbria in its integrity.

In the same year, 1041, the people of Worcester rose in insurrection against an unpopular tax, and the three great Earls, Siward

of Northumbria, Leofric of Mercia, and Godwine
of Kent, were directed to march thither to
suppress it. The was done chiefly at the
instigation of Ælfric, Archbishop of York, who
had caused their Bishop, Lyfric, to be deprived,
and himself appointed in his room, to hold the
see *in commendam* with York, but whom the
clergy of Worcester refused to recognise. The
Earls had no difficulty in suppressing the
revolt—indeed the rebels scarcely made any
stand against them ; but, with great barbarity,
they slaughtered the people, plundered their
habitations, burnt the city, and compelled
them to accept Ælfric as their Bishop.

The following year Hathacnut died, and was
succeeded by Eadwarde the Confessor, more fitted
for the cowl than the crown, when the three
Earls, the mightiest subjects of the realm,
divided the administration of the kingdom
amongst themselves ; Siward at this time held
likewise the Earldoms of Huntingdon and
Northampton, which were severed from Northumbria at his death.

In 1051, Count Eustace of Boulogne, on his
return from a visit to King Eadwarde, treated
the people of Dover with great insolence, who

fell upon him and his followers, and gave them a deservedly severe chastisement. Eustace demanded redress from the King, who commanded Earl Godwine to punish the Dover people, who, finding that Eustace had been the aggressor, asked that they might be heard in their defence, to which the King would not listen; then Godwine assumed a higher tone, and demanded the surrender of the Count to answer for his insolence. This enraged the King, who summoned Siward and Leofric to render assistance against the hostile designs of Godwine. They came to Gloucester, where a compromise was effected; but at a subsequent gemôt, held in London, Godwine and his family were banished.

The most creditable military effort of the many in which his sword had been drawn, and that which redounded the most to his glory, was the last of his life. In 1054, he was sent by King Eadwarde in command of an expedition into Scotland against the usurper, Macbeth, in favour of the young Prince, Malcolm Canmore, son of the murdered King Duncan. He was now the father of two sons by his first wife— Æthelfleda—Osbert, now approaching manhood,

E

and Waltheof, a boy, some years younger. The former he took with him to Scotland, to initiate him in the then deemed glorious art of war ; and a brave young fellow he proved himself to be, a worthy scion of the old stock. Siward attacked Scotland by land and sea, met the usurper and defeated him in a pitched battle, after which he caused Malcolm to be proclaimed King. It is sometimes stated that Macbeth was slain in the battle, which was not the case, as he escaped and held out for three years, maintaining a desultory series of fights with Malcolm, but was eventually slain in 1057. His son Osbert fell in the battle, fighting bravely, and when the news was brought to him, he eagerly inquired if his wounds were in front, and when told they were, said that he could not but rejoice, such a death being worthy of one sprung from his loins.

Shakspeare, not always true to history, in his tragedy of " Macbeth " thus gives the death of " Young Siward," as he calls Osbert :—He meets with Macbeth on the field, and, after some bandying of words, they fight, and Macbeth falls, after which Osbert rushes into the thick of the fight, and falls himself. When Siward is told that all his son's wounds are in front, he exclaims—

"Why, then, God's soldier is he !
Had I as many sons as I have hairs,
I would not wish them to a fairer death :
And so his knell is tolled."

Prince Malcolm observes—

"He's worth more sorrow,
And that I'll spend for him."

To which Siward replies—

"He's worth no more.
They say he parted well, and paid his score,
And so God be with him."

Henry of Huntingdon, speaking of Siward's death, says—"And so he passed away, as he believed, to Valhalla, to rejoin the great warriors of his race who had gone before," seeming to intimate, founded on the misconception of his identity with the Viking Siward—Barn, that he died in the old Scandinavian faith of Woden, which was not true, as he lived and died a Christian, such as Christians were then. He is supposed to have founded a church in York, dedicated to St. Olaf, the martyred King of Norway, and connected with it a fraternity of monks, the name of which, in the reign of William II., was changed into that of St. Mary the Virgin, and eventually became the famous and wealthy abbey of after-times, with a mitred abbot.   The ruins may now be seen in the grounds of the Museum.

He ruled his province with great firmness and some severity, necessary in his endeavours to curb the savage propensities of the people, and to establish a system of order and good government, and was bountiful to the Church, as some atonement, perhaps, for the crimes by which he rose to his high position.

Shortly after his return from his Scottish expedition, he was stricken with dysentery, which rapidly grew worse, and he lay in his viceregal mansion at York without hope of recovery. When he felt his last moments approaching he suddenly started up from his couch and exclaimed, "Let me not die the death of a cow! If it be not my fate to die gloriously on the field of battle, as my brave boy, Osbert, has done, with all his wounds in front, at least let me die in the guise of a warrior.   Don me my harness, place the helmet on my head, and gird my sword on my thigh.   It were a shame and disgrace that I, who have faced death in so many fields, should die ignominiously in bed.   Bring forth my battle-axe and shield, and place them by my side, that the ghosts of my warlike ancestry, who are looking down upon me now, may see me pass away from earth to join them in their everlasting home, with the semblance of the great warrior that I have been." And thus, seated on a chair, clothed in his armour, and supported in an upright posture by his attendants, he gave up the ghost, and was buried in his church of St. Olaf.

His son, Waltheof, being too young for the government of so important a province, it was given to Tosti, son of Earl Godwine, and brother of Harold, the future King; whilst Waltheof succeeded to the Earldoms of Huntingdon and Northampton, and eventually to that of Northumbria.

Phases in the Life of a Political Martyr.

IN the year 1055, there was a funeral in the Church of St. Olaf, York. The corpse was conveyed through the streets of the city with great barbaric splendour and pomp. The procession, consisting of stalwart and bronzed warriors, was strikingly illustrative of the dead hero. Swords flashed in the sun; armour, pikes, and battle-axes glittered; and captured pennons, with other trophies of war, were borne along in triumph. Although all these warriors were mourners, the chief, and, indeed, the only one of the blood who followed, was a stripling of fifteen, young in years, but displaying muscular proportions, a military bearing, and features betokening valour, determination of purpose, and invincible resolution in the accomplishment of his will. The warrior was laid in his tomb with all due ceremonial, the priests closed their books, the soldiers who had followed him to many a battlefield, gathered round the open grave to take a last look at his coffin, and then dispersed, whilst the young mourner returned to the vice-regal castle, which now seemed so solitary and desolate without the sound of his father's voice. The defunct warrior was stout old Siward, the Northumbrian Earl, who had scorned " to die the death of a cow," and the mourner who followed his remains was his sole surviving son, Waltheof; his elder son, Osbert, having been slain in battle. Eadward the Confessor was then King, and he, deeming Waltheof too young and inexperienced to rule so ungovernable a people as the Northumbrians, appointed Tosti, a younger son of Earl Godwine, and brother to Harold, afterwards King, to the Earldom. Tosti, however, ruled the people with such intolerable cruelty and oppression that the people of York broke into his mansion, plundered it, and murdered his house-carles; they then assembled in a folkgemôte and formally deposed him, electing Morkere of Mercia in his room. This was an illegal act, but the King, when he heard the circumstances of the case, confirmed it, as did also the Witan-Gemôte of Westminster. Morkere constituted Osulf, Waltheof's uncle, his deputy in Bernicia, on whose death he was succeeded by his brother, Gospatric.

John of Peterborough says that Waltheof was given the Earldoms of Huntingdon and Northampton at his father's death ; but as these were held by Tosti, the probability seems to be that he succeeded on the deposition of that Earl. Simeon of Durham says that he governed Bernicia as his father's deputy, but this seems improbable on account of his age, and is not confirmed by other authorities. On the accession of Harold, Tosti, in conjunction with Harold Hardrada, invaded Northumbria, but were defeated by Harold at Stamford Bridge. It was, however, the cause of the ruin of Harold, who, whilst banquetting at York in celebration of his victory, had news brought him that Duke William of Normandy had landed in Sussex, and he had to lead his army by forced marches to the south, arriving in the front of the fresh Norman troops footsore and wearied, and with the loss of many who had fallen out of the ranks during the march ; the result being his defeat and death, which might have been otherwise but for this fatal expedition to York. The brother Earls, Morkere of

Northumbria and Eadwine of Mercia, and Waltheof undertook to bring bodies of soldiers to his aid, but the former two stood aloof, from politic motives ; but Waltheof sent his contingent, if he were not present at the battle himself, which is uncertain.

Duke William was now King of England. London, with the south and east, had submitted at once, but it cost him some efforts to subjugate the west, and still more the north. He did, however, eventually make himself master of Yorkshire and the northern counties, built a castle at York, and placed therein William Malet as military governor of the city. The year after his accession, he found it necessary to visit his Norman Dukedom, when, fearing to leave behind him men so powerful, and whom he suspected of disaffection, he courteously invited Earls Eadwine, Morkere, and Waltheof, to accompany him as guests, who complied with his request, although they were perfectly aware that they were going as hostages for the good behaviour of their people during his absence. Soon after their return, the three Earls, under Earl Gospatric, made a demonstration in the north in favour of Eadgar, the Atheling, but were defeated, and fled to the court of Malcolm, in Scotland. William sent a herald to demand the fugitives, but the King declined giving them up.

In the year 1069, a Danish fleet of 240 vessels might be seen sailing up the Humber and Ouse. It was under the command of the Danish Princes Harold and Cnut, and had been joined at sea by a Scottish fleet under Gospatric and Waltheof. This formidable force landed near York, and entered the city amid the acclamations of the citizens. Malet was shut up in the Castle with a body of Norman troops, and had boastingly written to the King that he wanted no help, for he could hold it till domesday. Around the Castle walls were several houses, which Malet ordered to be fired, that they might not afford shelter to the enemy, but the fire spread further than he intended, consuming the greater portion of the city, the Cathedral, and Archbishop Egbert's magnificent library. It was whilst the flames were rising up with terrific grandeur from the Cathedral towers, and the houses were all ablaze or in ashes, that the confederates made their grand attack, captured the citadel, and put the garrison to the sword.

Waltheof performed prodigies of valour. It is recorded of him in a Danish saga—" The great Earl, with mighty arm and sinewy breast, stood by the gate of York (Castle) as the Normans came forth, their heads falling to the earth in succession beneath his battle-axe." Waltheof was appointed Governor of York, the English and Scots garrisoning it, whilst the Danes, in their ships, occupied the Trent and Ouse, to check the advance of William and his army.

It was not long before the King made his appearance before York and demanded its surrender.

Waltheof replied, " Take it if you can, for assuredly I will not surrender it while life lasts." The King then bribed the Danes to withdraw, by a large sum of money and permission to ravage the northern coasts, and invested the city. A breach was made in the walls, and William of Malmesbury says— "Waltheof, a man of great muscular strength and courage, stood in the breach, and killed a great number of Normans who attempted to enter." He states, also, that a battle was fought outside the walls, and that Waltheof was the victor. The siege lasted six months, and the city was reduced at last by famine, after which the King committed the horrible crime of laying waste the country from York to Durham so effectually that for nine years neither spade nor plough was put in the ground, and the miserable survivors who escaped his sword were com pelled to eat the most loathsome food to sustain life.

Gospatric, Earl of Northumbria, and Waltheof fled to Scotland, but afterwards tendered their submission to the King, the latter in person, the other by proxy. Waltheof was a man of immense power and influence as Lord of Hallam- shire, Malton, and many another broad manor in Yorkshire and other counties, and was, besides, a skilful warrior and brave soldier, and the King, admiring his qualities, longed to win him over as his liege man. He therefore pardoned him, restored him to his Earldoms, and added thereto that of Northumbria, from which he had deposed Gospatric. Moreover, he gave him in marriage his niece, Judith, daughter of Eudes, Earl of Champagne, thinking thus to make sure of his loyalty.

Soon after he entered upon his new Earldom

he committed a crime which is a blot upon his name, but which was considered justifiable in that age. A deadly feud existed between the descendants of Ughtred and those of one Thorbrand of York. Thorbrand was the enemy of the father of the second wife of Ughtred, who only obtained her hand by undertaking to kill him, but was murdered himself by Thorbrand. Earl Ealdred then, in retaliation, assassinated Thorbrand, and was in turn killed by Carl, son of Thorbrand, and a series of murders followed, which were completed by a wholesale massacre of the sons of Carl by Waltheof, when they were feasting at the house of their elder brother at Settrington, two only escaping.

There was a great feast in the eastern counties to celebrate the marriage of Ralph, Earl of Suffolk, with Emma, daughter of Roger, son of William, Earl of Hereford, and Waltheof was one of the guests. This marriage had been prohibited by the King, who was now in Normandy, and advantage was taken of his absence to consummate it, which was, in the eye of the law, a treasonable act. After the dinner, the conversation turned upon the tyranny of

King William, and, as the guests became heated
with wine, they framed a plot to depose him, and
place one of themselves as King in his room, the
rest to be his proximate peers. Waltheof is said
to have taken the oath on compulsion, but the
following morning repented of having done so,
and went to Archbishop Lanfrane for absolution,
who advised him to go to the King, explain the
matter, and implore his pardon. He had,
however, foolishly mentioned it to his wife
Judith, who, wishing to get rid of "the Saxon
churl" and marry a Norman, sent an exaggerated
account of the conspiracy to her uncle, with the
intimation that her husband was most deeply
implicated in it. Waltheof went to Normandy,
revealed the plot to the King, and asked his
forgiveness for the part he had been compelled
to take in it, who assured him of pardon, and
they returned to England together.

The King, however, who had now for some time
looked upon Waltheof as too powerful for a
subject, thought this a favourable opportunity
to get rid of him, and when he arrived in
England, committed him to prison at Winchester.
He then caused him to be arraigned at the
Pentecostal gemôte, on a charge of treasonable

conspiracy, and he was condemned to death. A few days after he was brought out into the market-place at Winchester, and there beheaded; the first instance, says Kennett, of decapitation in England. Ingulphus says that Judith might have saved him, but she desired his death that she might marry again, and afterwards experienced feelings of remorse for her cruelty. She subsequently fell into disgrace with her uncle for refusing to marry one who was lame. Her name appears in Domesday Book as Lady of the Manors of Hallam, Sheffield, and Attercliffe.

By his wife Judith he had issue, three daughters, co-heiresses—Matilda, who married first Simon de St. Liz, and secondly, David I., King of Scotland, thus conveying the Earldom of Huntingdon to the Scottish Royal Family; Alice, who married Richard Fitz Gilbert, whose granddaughter and heiress married Richard Fitz Ooth, from whom was Robert Fitz Ooth, who claimed the Earldom of Huntingdon on the failure of the Scottish male line, and who is generally supposed to be identical with the outlaw Robin Hood; and Judith, who married first Ralph de Toney, secondly Robert, son of

Richard de Tonbridge, from whom descended the Barons and Earls Fitzwalter, the Earldom becoming extinct, and the Barony falling in abeyance in 1753, the latter being called out in 1868, in the person of Sir Brook William Brydges, fifth Baronet of, County Kent.

The Murderer's Bride.

IT was on a beautiful evening in June, when the thirteenth century was but a few years old, and when John wore the crown of England, that a girl of some twenty summers was seated in a vaulted room of a ruinous old Saxon castle, surrounded by her bower-maidens, chattering and laughing, and busily employed on some embroidery work. The castle stood on a slight eminence, some three or four miles from the sea-coast of Yorkshire, and commanding a glorious view of the uplands of Cleveland, the wide expanse of ocean, the only recently completed towers of St. Hilda's Abbey, as they stood proudly on the beetling cliff, and the clustering of fishermen's huts on the margin of the bay below, then called the village of Presteby, formerly Streoneshalh, and now Whitby. It had been built by the half-mythical Saxon noble, Wada, as a defence against the marauding Picts, who came over the border, and

F

more particularly against the Danish Vikings, who were wont to land at Flamborough, and harry the land. In the year 867, they had destroyed the Lady Hilda's monastery, and it lay in ruins until after the Conquest, when it was re-built and re-endowed by William de Percy, ancestor of the potent Earls of Northumberland, and about half a century before the period of our narrative, it had been again pillaged and the country laid waste by a Norwegian fleet. But, amid all these storms, the old castle built by Wada held its own, although it now showed in its features the ravages of time and the marks of the batterings it had undergone from the hands of a succession of foes, in the shape of fallen towers, crumbling walls, and decayed battlements. After the Conquest, the castle and barony were granted by the King to Nigel Fossard, a soldier who had fought for him at Hastings, and from whose family it passed, after two or three generations, to Robert de Turnham, by marriage with Johanna, heiress of the Fossards. They were now dead, and slept side by side within the sacred precincts of St. Hilda, having left an only child—Isabel—as heiress, and now mistress of the ruined old fortress, and the domain of pasture and moorland lying round it; the same fair girl whom we find seated at her embroidery frame. The apartment in which the youthful group were assembled was the Lady Isabel's bower, very different, however, from a modern boudoir, being of the usual Saxon type. The walls and vaulted roof were of roughly-hewn stone, with a low, stunted column in the centre, and rounded arches, slightly decorated with a zigzag ornamentation, and on one side was an unglazed opening to admit the light, more like a loophole than a window. On the walls, suspended from tenter-hooks, were arras, picturing the miracles of St. Hilda, which served to give some semblance of comfort and cheerfulness to the room; and the other furniture consisted of a table, or board resting on two trestles, and half a dozen cross-legged stools.

Sounds of merriment and laughter echoed from the roof, as the maidens plied their needles, the buoyancy of their youthful spirits, and the outlook into what appears like a fairyland of the future, imparting a sunshine which is the happy privilege of youth, but is denied to more mature age. Yet, in the midst of all this joyous mirth, Isabel occasionally sighed, as disquieting thoughts passed through her mind. She was left in an

unprotected solitude, and although the good
Abbot of St. Hilda's had been her father's friend,
and had promised him on his death-bed to watch
over her and aid her by his counsel, he could not
supply the place of father and mother, of whom
she had been bereft, or of sister or brother, a
companionship she had never experienced. She
had already begun to taste the cares and anxieties
of her position, and looked forward with some
degree of apprehension, having learnt that the
King, as absolute lord of the soil of England, had
the right and power to dispose of the hands of
heiresses of any portion of that soil which was
only held of him by baronial or knightly tenure.

"The sun goes down apace," said Isabel, rising
and going to look forth from the window, "fold
up the altar-cloth, we shall have time to complete
the embroidery before the obit of St. Hilda." She
gazed out upon the sea, sparkling with the glitter
of the setting sun, and looked upon the abbey
tower on the cliff, still radiant with brightness—
an out-post, as it seemed to her, of the realms of
heaven, and she felt a peaceful calm steal over her
mind. Suddenly her eyes gleamed with joy, and
her heart began to throb with passionate gladness.
These emotions were awakened by the sight of a

youth of noble bearing, pacing with rapid steps
the road leading to the castle.   This youth was
Jasper de Percy, a scion of the afterwards illustrious house of that name.   He had long been
affianced to Isabel, with the consent and full
approbation of their parents, and they loved each
other dearly and passionately.   It was not long
ere he was ushered into her presence by the old
seneschal of the castle, but with their soft
whisperings we have nothing to do, save that we
know they consisted of protestations of eternal
love and anticipations of a happy future.   Whilst
they were together the sun went down, and, as
the bell of compline rang out sweetly over the
water, they knelt together and uttered their
evening prayer to the Holy Virgin, after which he
departed.

"Pax vobiscum!" said the Abbot, as he entered
the room soon after, "how fares it with my
daughter?" She replied that she was well in health,
but somewhat disquieted in soul, and told him
what she had heard about the King having the
disposal of the hands of heiresses, and asking him
if it were so.   He explained the law to her, and
knowing and approving of her love for young Percy,
expressed a hope that His Majesty would not inter-

fere in her case, but, added he, "King John is a bad man, unscrupulous in his actions, and an arch-heretic, even to the defying of the Holy Father at Rome—the Vicegerent of God upon earth, saying that he will allow no foreign priest to meddle in his dominion." After some further conversation, Isabel knelt at his feet, confessed her little faults, received absolution, and the Abbot returned to St. Hilda's. So the days and weeks went on in their usual routine, with nothing to disturb their serenity, until at length a thunderbolt, as it were, fell suddenly in the midst of the little community, utterly destroying all their fond hopes of happiness.

The scene now changes to Normandy. King Henry II. of England had four sons, of whom William, the eldest, d.v.p., and Richard, the second, succeeded, who d.s.p. The third, Geoffrey, married Constance, daughter and heiress of Conan le Petit, Duke of Bretagne and Earl of Richmond, and had issue, Arthur, who was heir to the throne of England on the death of his uncle Richard, but, being absent in Brittany, John, fourth son of Henry, usurped the throne, and when Philip of France espoused the cause of Arthur, he invaded France with an army, to

maintain the position he had assumed, and with
the intention of removing the obstacle to his legal
right to the throne. He captured his nephew,
after patching up a peace with King Philip, and
sent him to Falaise, with instructions to Hubert
de Burgh to put his eyes out. Hubert, however,
compassionated the boy, and saved him from that
fate, upon which King John removed Arthur
from his custody, and had him taken to Rouen,
and placed in safe keeping. The midnight bell at
St. Ouen had rung out over the Norman city,
and, saving that, all was still in its tortuous
streets, excepting the footsteps of three persons
going down to the river-side. They went along
stealthily, one of them, a boy, with seeming
reluctance, and who appeared to be expostulating
with the two men who urged him along. " I tell
thee, boy," said he who was evidently the chief
of the company, " that thou shalt be Duke of
Bretagne and Earl of Richmond, and we are but
taking thee to a place of safety wherein to abide
until these untoward matters that agitate the
realm of France can be arranged." " But my
crown, the crown of England, my inheritance!"
commenced the boy as they arrived at the water's
side, when the two men forced him into a boat

and pushed it off upon the Seine, and it glided down the river beyond the confines of the city. The leader of the party was King John, and the other his esquire, an ill-favoured bully, with an evil cast of the eye, a Poictevin by birth, and called, in derision, Peter de Malo-lacu, afterwards softened down to Maulac, and eventually to De Mauley. He was one of the tools and evil counsellors of John, and was ever ready to commit any crime provided he were well paid for it. Their companion was the boy Prince, Arthur. The night was dreary and murky, and the wind wailed a mournful cadence through the trees, well befitting the contemplated deed of blood. The boat had passed some distance down the river, and Arthur, fearing some foul design, was imploring his uncle to be taken back to Rouen, when the Poictevin, in reply to a signal from the King, suddenly plunged his dagger up to the hilt in the boy's breast, and at the same moment seized him by the legs, and pitched him over the side of the boat into the river, to pass down to the sea with the ebbing tide.

" 'Twas well done," said John to his companion in guilt, "that obstacle to our ambition is removed for ever; and as for thee, Peter, thou shalt be great amongst the nobles of our realm. It will be hard if I cannot find an heiress lacking a husband, and thou shalt be a baron of England."

Again are we among the merry hills and dales of Cleveland. The summer has passed away, the leaves of autumn have fallen, the fierce blasts of the wintry winds of North Yorkshire have toned down into the gentle gales of spring, and a glad sunshine pervades land and sea. But there is wailing and lamentation within the walls of Wada's old castle, and saddened hearts beneath the shadow of St. Hilda's tower. The marriage of Isabel and Jasper had been arranged, and nothing was wanting for its consummation but the sanction of the King. A messenger had been despatched to the Court of John to obtain his consent, but he replied that it could not be, as he had other views in regard to the heiress, and purposed, by giving her hand to a brave warrior of Poictou, to raise her to a dignity far above anything ever attained by the Turnhams or the Fossards; in short, that he intended giving her in marriage to his friend and companion-in-arms, Peter de Maulac. Hence those tears and lamentations, as there was no resisting the King's will.

A few months, and there stood before the altar of St. Hilda, decorated with the embroidery from the deft fingers of Isabel and her bower-maidens, an ill-assorted couple. On the one side a forbidding-looking man, with a ferocious cast of countenance and an eye of ill omen; on the other, a gentle, delicate girl, of symmetrical figure and beautifully chiselled features, but pale as a corpse, and with eyes swollen and bloodshot with weeping. Nevertheless, it mattered not, the mandate of the King must be obeyed, and they became man and wife.

Peter de Mauley, as he now chose to style himself, thus became, by right of his wife, feudal lord of Isabel's demesnes, situated at Egton, Juby-Park-Houses, and Newbiggin, near Whitby; Mauley Cross, near Pickering; Bainton, near Driffield; Ellerton, near Pocklington; and Seaton, near Hornsea; but the King compelled him to pay for the livery of these estates a fine of 7,000 marks. He built a new castle near the old one, and called it, from the beauty of the situation, Moult-grace, but which the people, in consequence of his oppression, transformed, by the change of a single letter, into Moult-grave, since then corrupted into Mulgrave. He was a firm adherent of John in his troubles with the Pope and the Barons, and was rewarded for his services with other considerable grants of lands, the Sheriffdoms of Dorset and Somerset, and, under Henry III., with the Governorship of Sherborne Castle. He died in 1221, and the ill-fated Isabel pre-deceased him, whose body he buried in Meaux Abbey, near Beverley, giving with it a grant of land.

They had a son—Peter—who succeeded, who was followed by six other Peters in unbroken succession, all of whom enjoyed the estates, excepting the seventh, who died v.p. The fourth was created a baron by writ of summons in 1295 ; but Peter the eighth, fourth in the barony, dying without issue in 1415, the dignity fell in abeyance between his sisters and co-heiresses—Constance, who married, first, William Fairfax, secondly, Sir John Bigot, and who succeeded to Moult-grave, and Elizabeth, who married George Salvin. The title was revived in 1838, as a barony by patent, in the person of the Hon. W. F. Spencer Ponsonby, third son of the Earl of Bessborough, a descendant, through females, of Elizabeth Salvin; but the old barony by writ still lies in abeyance among the representatives of the above co-heiresses.

The death of Prince Arthur is still shrouded in mystery, the English chroniclers giving different versions of it, and Shakspeare representing him as being killed by a fall from the walls of his prison when attempting to escape ; but the French historians, who are more likely to be correct, coincide in attributing it to the hand of Peter de Malo-lacu, in the presence of John, or even to that of the King himself.

The Earldom of Wiltes.

HE famous Yorkshire family of Le Scrope, or Scroop, is one of the most illustrious in the peerage roll of England; not, however, for the number and dignity of their titles, which only amounted to five of lesser rank, two of which are extinct, one dormant, and two in abeyance, but, for the many eminent and influential men sprung from the race, who have distinguished themselves in the State, at the King's Council table, in the Church, at the Bar, on the battlefield, and in the walks of literature.   During three centuries, from Edward II. to Charles I., there have been of the Scropes—two Earls, twenty Barons, one Baronet, one Archbishop, four Bishops, one Lord Chancellor, four Lord Treasurers, five Knights of the Garter, several Knights Banneret, many Wardens of the Scottish Marches, three immortalised in the pages of Shakspeare, one, "Keen Lord Scrope," in the ballad of "Kinmont Willie," and another in the ballad of "Flodden Field."

They were originally of Normandy, and in the reign of William I., Osborne Fitz-Richard, their first English ancestor, held several manors in the Western counties. The first mention of them in connection with Yorkshire is in 1287, when they held eight carucates of land at Bolton, where they built Bolton Castle. They rose rapidly in importance, ramifying in various directions, mainly into two great branches, those of Masham and Bolton, subsequently having mansions and domains at Bolton Castle; Clifton Castle, Masham; Danby Hall, Middleham; Upsall Castle, Thirsk; Croft-on-the-Tees, Ellerton-upon-Swale, Spennithorne, and South Kilvington; and are now represented by a junior branch, seated at Danby-super-Yore.

Henry, seventh Baron Scrope, of Bolton, was one of the heroes of Flodden, whose valour is sung in the ballad of Flodden Field. John, eighth Baron, was implicated in the rebellion of the Pilgrimage of Grace, but escaped the death of a traitor. Henry, ninth Baron, had charge of Mary Queen of Scots, at Bolton. Henry, third Baron Scrope, of Masham, was executed for treason, as was also Richard Scrope, Archbishop of York.

The time in which Sir William Scrope, K.G., Earl of Wiltes, and King of the Isle of Man, lived, that of the reign of Richard II., was one of the most eventful in the history of England. Richard, son of the Black Prince, was born in 1367, and succeeded to the throne of his grandfather, Edward III., at ten years of age, in 1377, the government being vested in twelve councillors, his uncles being excluded therefrom. He displayed signs of vigour and ability during the insurrection under Wat Tyler and Jack Straw, when he met the rebels in Smithfield, on which occasion the former was killed by Lord Mayor Walworth; and in his invasion of Scotland, in 1385, when he penetrated as far as Aberdeen, and burnt Edinburgh, Perth, and Dundee; but afterwards he threw himself into the arms of favourites, which excited the jealousy of his uncles, when the Duke of Gloucester was chosen head of the Council, and the parliament, called "wonderful," summoned under his auspices, put two of his favourites to death, and confiscated the property of the rest. When he reached the age of twenty-two he threw off the trammels of guardianship, and for some time ruled his kingdom with justice, but he possessed not the necessary vigour to cope with the turbulent spirits by whom he was surrounded, and still permitted himself to be governed by favourites, of whom Sir William Scrope was one.

Sir William might almost be said to be born a courtier. His father, Richard, first Baron of Bolton; his uncle, Geoffrey, first Baron of Masham; and his maternal uncle, Michael de la Pole, son of a Hull merchant, and created Earl of Suffolk by Richard II., were all foremost men about the Court in military, diplomatic, legislative, judicial, and other capacities. His father was a statesman of rare talent, and resigned his chancellorship in 1380, in consequence of the anger of the young King at his protests against the lavish grants he made to his favourites. Pole, Earl of Suffolk, and De Vere, Duke of Ireland, with Brember, Mayor of London, and Tresilian, were the King's favourites in his early days, but in 1388, Gloucester and the confederated Barons attacked them, compelled the two former to take to flight, and put to death the two latter. After their dispersion, Sir William Scrope became one of the principal advisers and favourites of the King, who loaded

him with honours and wealth. He was constituted Seneschal of Acquitaine in 1383 ; Governor
of the town and castle of Cherbourg in 1385 ;
and Governor of Queensborough Castle in the
same year; was appointed Vice-Chamberlain of
the Household in 1393, and Lord Chamberlain in
1395. He was sent as Ambassador to France to
negotiate the marriage of the King, in 1395,
and to treat for peace, in 1397. He was
nominated Justicier of Chester, North Wales,
and Flint, in 1397, and in the same year
Surveyor of the Forests in Cheshire. In 1397,
he was created Earl of Wiltes; the following
year had charge of the castle of Guisnes ; and in
1399, was appointed guardian of the realm during
the absence of the King in Ireland. He was a
faithful servant and attached friend to his
master, and laid down his life in his service.

The causes of the deposition and death of
Richard were his weak character and his
obnoxious mode of government, through favourites
and evil advisers, which were accelerated by the
ambition and revenge of his cousin Henry, Duke
of Hereford, son of John of Gaunt, Duke of
Lancaster. The Duke of Hereford had a quarrel
with Mowbray, Duke of Norfolk, each accusing

G

the other of treason, and the King consented that
the matter should be decided by combat at
Coventry, but when the lists were opened and
the combatants mounted, lance in hand, ready to
commence the fight, the King commanded them
to desist, and arbitrarily condemned Norfolk to
banishment from the realm for life, and Hereford
for ten years, the latter being granted the
privilege of taking possession, through his
attorney, of any inheritances that might fall to
him during his absence.   Whilst he was abroad
his father, the Duke of Lancaster, died, and the
King, in violation of his promise, took possession
of his widely-spread lands in Yorkshire and
elsewhere, including Leeds, Kippax, Almondbury,
and many another manor in the county.   Henry,
now Duke of Lancaster, had speedy intelligence
of this from his attorney, and gathering a few
followers together, took shipping for England,
and landed at Ravenspurn, in Holderness, at the
mouth of the Humber.   His ostensible motive in
coming to England, and perhaps his real
intention, was simply to obtain possession of his
inheritance, with, possibly, some vague ideas of
vengeance for his banishment.   But, as he passed
through Yorkshire, he was joined by the Percies

and other powerful families, who welcomed him back to England, and the people flocked round his standard, so that when he approached London he found himself at the head of a considerable army, and then he threw off his disguise, and proclaimed that he had come to deliver the kingdom from the evil advisers of the Crown. The King had gone to Ireland to subdue an insurrection, and had left the Earl of Wiltes as guardian of the realm, who, on hearing of the march of Lancaster towards London, fled, with others, to Bristol, hoping to join the King there on his return from Ireland. The Duke followed them thither, laid siege to the castle, " where at length," says Walsingham, " William le Scrope, John Busby, and Henry Grene, were taken prisoners, and they were forthwith, on the morrow, beheaded, at the outcry of the populace." The Duke had now fully resolved upon striking for the Crown, although he was not the legitimate heir, even if Richard were removed, and it was his usurpation which gave rise to the subsequent War of the Roses. In furtherance of his project, he considered it desirable to win over the citizens of London, and in order to conciliate those who were opposed to the favourites, and terrify those

who were friendly to the King and his government, he sent thither the heads of Scrope, Busby,
and Grene, in a basket, with a letter, in which he
said—"I beg of you to let me know if you will
be on my side or not, and I care not which, for I
have people enough to fight all the world for one
day. But take in good part the present I have
sent you," etc. This produced the effect he
wished for, as the Londoners at once espoused his
cause. The King was soon after captured, sent
to Pontefract Castle, and there murdered, after a
formal deposition ; and Henry, with the consent
of Parliament, assumed the crown. He called a
Parliament together, who, in the first year of his
reign, passed an Act of Attainder and Confiscation against the Earl of Wiltes and other of
Richard's friends ; and it was assumed that the
earldom thus became extinct, although legally it
only became dormant, and presents one of the
most curiously complicated and interesting cases
that ever came before the Court of Heralds or
the House of Lords, paralleled only, perhaps,
in interest by the famous Scrope-Grosvenor
heraldic dispute, between Sir Richard Scrope, the
Earl's father, and Sir Robert Grosvenor, as to
the right to bear "azure a bend or" on their

shields of arms, in which 400 witnesses of the highest rank appeared in evidence.

The patent of the Earldom was thus made out :—" We, considering the probity, the wise and provident circumspection, and the illustriousness of manners and birth of our beloved and trusty William le Scrope, Chevalier, and willing deservedly to exalt him by the prerogative of honour, do create him in Parliament to be Earl of Wiltes ; and do invest him with the style, name, and honour of the place aforesaid, by the girding of the sword, to have to him and his heirs-male for ever. And in order that the Earl and his heirs aforesaid, for the decency of so great a name and honour, may be the better and the more honourably able to support the burdens incumbent on the same, of our special grace we have given and granted, and by this charter confirm, to the Earl and his heirs aforesaid, £20 to be received every year out of the issues of the county of Wilton, by the hands of the sheriff of the county for ever." The patent was made out in this way, with remainder to his heirs-male, because, although married, he had no issue by whom it might descend lineally, and it would thus pass downward in the family through his collateral heirs, his brothers or their children. In 1859, Simon Thomas Scrope, of Danby, claimed the dormant Earldom, as heir-general of the grantee, on the ground that the attainder was invalid, and the case occupied the consideration of the House of Lords for ten years. In the first place, the question arose whether by "heirs-general," collateral descendants were meant, which was decided in the affirmative, and the claimant then proved to the satisfaction of the House that he was the heir-general. It was then contended that the attainder was invalid, as taking up arms in defence of a reigning Sovereign could not by any possibility be construed into treason; but, on the other hand, it was argued that the attainder was legal, as it was an Act of the first Parliament called by Henry. But it was shown that before Henry's assumption of the crown, whilst the King was in captivity, he made grants of the Earl's lands and goods in the name of the King, using Richard's name and seal for the purpose, as he did also in issuing writs for the summoning of a new Parliament, which were ante-dated so as to appear to have been issued by the King, and this Parliament it was which passed the Act of the Attainder. "This, of course," as Elsynge says, "was entirely illegal, for as the Earl had been illegally executed, without the pretence, or the possibility of a pretence, of any legal charge or lawful trial, there could be nothing to affect the legal rights which devolved upon his heirs, and a murder could hardly create a forfeiture." Further, it was shown that all the attainders of the Parliament of Henry were reversed by the first Parliament of Edward IV., therefore, even if the attainder had been perfectly legal, it became null and void by the subsequent reversal, and consequently the title was now lying dormant, and belonged to the heir-general of Sir William Scrope. This seems to be very simple, clear, and logical, but the Lords of the nineteenth century thought otherwise, and gave their decision that an Act of Parliament of the fourteenth century should be held to be valid, simply because it was an Act of Parliament, even although reversed by a subsequent Act, and that, consequently, the claim could not be admitted. The legitimate heir to the Earldom is, therefore, debarred from enjoying his title. But if the principle which operated adversely to his claim were to be set in motion retrospectively, many a proud coronet, even amongst those who voted against the claim, would fall to the ground.

It has been said by some authorities that Sir William was not the son of Richard, first Baron Scrope of Bolton, but his nephew, and son of Henry, first Baron Scrope of Masham.

He purchased, *circa* 1393, of William de Montacute, the sovereignty of the Isle of Man, the lord of the island at that time possessing the right of being crowned and styled king, although subject to the King of England.

At the time of the execution of the Earl, his brother Richard was Archbishop of York, who is represented by Walsingham, as having been "a pious and devout man, incomparably learned, of singular integrity, and of a goodly and amiable personage," and was so grieved at the murder of his brother, and so exasperated against the usurper Bolingbroke, that he entered into conspiracy with the Earl of Northumberland, who had been alienated from the King, and had lost his son (Hotspur) at the battle of Shrewsbury, and with Mowbray, Earl of Norfolk, son of the banished Earl, to dethrone King Henry. The standard of revolt, emblazoned with the five wounds of Christ, was raised at Shipton, near York, around which 20,000 Yorkshiremen ranged themselves. The Archbishop imprudently made known his intentions too openly, by fixing papers to church doors, charging the King with usurpation, perjury, sacrilege, and murder; 'by sending circulars to other counties calling upon the people to take up arms for his dethronement; and preaching three sermons denouncing him as a *pseudo* King, and a traitor to his sovereign. The King, of course, soon heard of these proceedings, and sent Prince John, afterwards Duke of Bedford, and the Earl of Westmoreland, with 30,000 men, to put down the insurrection. They found the conspirators so securely entrenched in the forest of Galtres that they deemed it most prudent to resort to a stratagem. By means of flattery and false promises they allured the Archbishop from his shelter, and immediately arrested him for high treason, taking him first to Pontefract and then to Bishopthorpe. The King directed the famous Judge Gascoigne to try and sentence him, who refused, saying that a Peer must be tried by his Peers. Judge Fulthorpe, who was less scrupulous, was then appointed, and, with scarcely the formality of a trial, condemned him to death.

" Presently after, he was set upon an ill-favoured jade, his face towards its tail, and was carried with great scorn to a field hard by, where his head was stricken off by a fellow that did his office very ill, not being able to decapitate with less than five strokes." He was looked upon as a martyr by the people, who flocked in crowds to pray at his tomb and place of execution, which was forbidden by the King by proclamation, and the Pope excommunicated all who were concerned in his death. (See " The Loyal Martyr, 1722." Maydestone's "History of the Martyrdom of Archbishop Scrope." "A Narrative of the Decollation of Archbishop Scrope, by Thos. Gascoigne, D.D.," in MS. in the Bod. Lib.; and "A Declaration of Archbishop Scrope against the Government of Henry IV." in Ang. Sec., vol. 2.)

Black-faced Clifford.

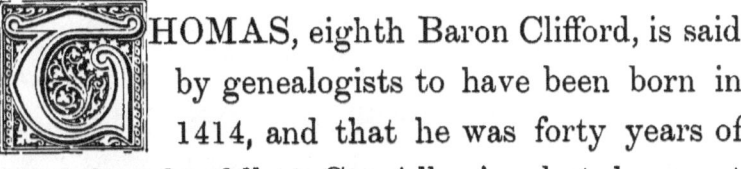HOMAS, eighth Baron Clifford, is said by genealogists to have been born in 1414, and that he was forty years of age when he fell at St. Alban's; but he must have been nearer fifty than forty, as his son John, ninth Baron, was born in 1430, when he would be but sixteen years of age; but marriages were contracted early then. His daughter, Elizabeth, was married at six years of age to Sir William Plumpton, who, dying soon after, she was re-married to his brother, her father stipulating that "they should not ligge together" until she had arrived at the age of eighteen. He was a portly, soldierly-looking figure, with a commanding presence, and a tone of voice calculated to ensure obedience to his commands. He had spent the greater part of his life, since the dawn of manhood, in the wars of France; was greatly applauded for his capture of Pontoise by a clever stratagem, in 1438, and

two years afterwards won equal admiration for
the skill and bravery with which he defended
it against the troops of King Charles VII., and
in 1445, he was entrusted with the high honour
of escorting to England, Margaret of Anjou, the
bride of Henry VI.

John, his son, was somewhat different,
possessing neither the martial figure, the open
countenance, nor the genial manner of his father.
His frame was more slenderly proportioned, his
face presented rather a scowl than a smile, and
his temperament inclined to a moroseness and
brooding, which rendered him cruel in war
and disagreeable amongst his private friends.

It was a beautiful May morning in the year
1455; the sun was shining brightly in the
Vale of Craven. Breakfast was spread in the
great hall of the castle of the Cliffords. On the
daïs at the upper end, sat, at the cross table,
Thomas, Lord Clifford, and his wife, the Lady
Joan, a daughter of Thomas, Lord Dacre, of
Gillesland; his son John, with his wife, Margaret,
daughter of Henry Bromflete; Baron Vesey; and
the Prior of Bolton, who had come over on
his mule to be present on this occasion. Down
the centre of the hall stretched the long table of

oaken planks resting on trestles, with benches on each side, on which were seated the knights of the fees of Skipton, esquires, the priests of the chapel, the secretary, the treasurer, the seneschal, the constable, and other of the higher officials of the castle, with others of meaner degree, all ranged higher or lower, above or below the salt, according to their rank. The tables were loaded with substantial fare— huge joints of beef, mutton, brawn, and venison ; saltfish, fresh herrings, and eels, with manchetts of bread in trenchers, interspersed with foaming flagons of ale and pewter tankards of sack. There was rudely cooked plenty, and keen appetites to overlook the deficiency of delicacies.

The conversation on the daïs turned upon the great topic of the day—the manifest aspiration of Richard, Duke of York, to the Crown of England, and the deposition of the imbecile and monkish-minded King Henry VI. Henry of Bolingbroke, son of John of Gaunt, fourth son of Edward, had usurped the throne of his cousin, Richard II., and had been succeeded by his son, Henry V., and his grandson, Henry VI., which usurpation gave rise to the desolating War of the Roses, now breaking out, and it could not be denied that Richard had a better claim, as the representative, through Anne, his mother, of the Duke of Clarence, than Henry had, as representative of the Duke of Lancaster.

"The summons from the King arrived a week ago," said Lord Clifford in reply to the Prior, "and you will perceive, Holy Father, that I have lost no time in obeying it."

"And a fine body of men you have gathered together," said the Prior, "the flower of Craven, whom it would be difficult to match for rude bravery and devotion to the will of their lord."

"True," replied Clifford, "but we have opposed to us the men of the Vale of Mowbray, under the Duke of Norfolk, and the stout men-at-arms of Middleham, the followers of Warwick and Salisbury, all Yorkshiremen, not less obstinately brave than those of Craven, to say nothing of the Durham retainers of the Nevilles from Raby. But then we shall have the powerful assistance of the Percys, with their troops from Topcliffe and Leckonfield and Wressle, so that it must be a fierce and bloody contest. I count but little upon the men of the south and the west of

England; it will be the valour of the north which shall decide it."

"Indeed, my lord," answered the Prior, "I foresee a long and bloody war, when such powerful competitors are pitted against each other, and I mourn over the thousands of desolated homesteads in Merry England, as it is wont to be called; merry, alas! I fear not, for many a long day to come."

"Have you had any further tidings, sir," inquired the younger Clifford, "of the movements of Richard of York!"

"Nothing," replied his father, "but that he has raised his standard on the borders of Wales, and is marching with his troops upon London, to demand justice upon Somerset; and further, I have received information that Salisbury, Warwick, and Mowbray, are hastening to join him. But we must not waste more time; we must perform a long march before sunset."

A short service was held, and mass said in the chapel before the leaders, by the Prior, and the head priest of the chapel extemporised a religious service in the courtyard to the soldiers, who stood bareheaded, and listened devoutly. In those days the lower classes, however rough and barbarous they might be, implicitly believed what was told them by the priests, without any dogmatic scruples whatever, believing that the shriving of the priest or monk cleared off all old scores of sin, and they might, without compunction, commence a fresh score; the sum and substance of their religion being to serve their feudal lord faithfully, accept the dogmas of the priest, and contribute according to their means to the money-chests of the Church and the monastery.

There was but scant leave-taking; the women of that time were so accustomed to parting with their husbands and sons for the French and Scottish wars, that they looked upon it as a matter of course. Outside the walls was a gathering of the wives, children, and sweethearts of the rank and file, with whom there were some tender leave-takings from those, so many of whom they would never more see, and who, despite their rough exterior, possessed within them hearts beating with affection and tenderness towards the cheerers of their cottage firesides.

The Royalists of Craven made but slow progress as they wended their way southward.

It was not until after some ten days' marching along rough roads, entangled woods, the fording of rivers, and tramping through morasses, that Lord Clifford and the men of Craven found themselves on the borders of Hertfordshire. Here they met with a messenger from the King, with information that Henry and Somerset, with an army, small in number, but composed chiefly of nobles and knights, men of experience and valour, had come forth from London to meet the Yorkists, and would await Lord Clifford's arrival at Watford, bidding him to speed with all haste to that rendezvous. Lord Clifford and his son at this summons spurred on their chargers, leaving the troops to follow. They found the King occupying a house in the small town, and in conference with the Duke of Somerset, who had been nominated by the Queen to the Generalship-in-chief of the forces; they were admitted to the presence at once, and were cordially received by Henry, Lord Clifford being high in his favour. The Yorkshire contingent entered the town soon after, with their banners displayed and trumpets sounding, and pitched their tents alongside those of the King's army. A council of war was called in the

H

evening, and Lord Clifford had the gratification of meeting there his uncle Henry, second Earl of Northumberland, now sixty years of age, King Henry V. having reversed the attainder of his grandfather, for the Shrewsbury and Bramham affairs, and restored him to the Percy estates and dignities, since which he had won distinction by sharing in the glory of Agincourt. At this council it was determined to march, on the following morning, upon St. Alban's, as it was ascertained from scouts that Richard of York, between whom and Somerset there was bitter enmity, was marching in that direction with an army he had gathered round him at Ludlow, which had been augmented on the road by the contingents of his sympathisers, and was supposed to outnumber the forces ranged under the Lancastrian banner.

The following morning the tents around Watford were struck by daylight; the troops breakfasted, and, with banners flying and trumpets sounding, they commenced their march towards St. Alban's. Sir Philip Wentworth carried the Royal standard; and with the King, as a guard of honour, were Humphrey, Duke of Buckingham, and his son, Earl Stafford; Henry

Percy, Earl of Northumberland; James Butler, Earl of Wiltshire; Thomas, Lord Clifford; and other nobles of the first rank.

As the army approached St. Alban's, they perceived the uplands in front of them covered with armed men, moving rapidly along towards the old Roman city, in battle array. On seeing this, the Lancastrians halted, set up the Royal standard, with Lord Clifford and his Craven men to guard the barriers. The Duke of Buckingham was sent to demand of the Duke of York why he thus appeared before his Sovereign. Duke Richard replied that he was loyal to the King, sought only for justice upon Somerset, and would at once lay down his arms if he would surrender him to be dealt with according to the laws of the kingdom. The King, on receiving this message, displayed unwonted spirit, and replied that "he would as soon give up his crown as deliver up either Somerset or the meanest soldier in his camp to the mercy of the Yorkists." This answer was final, and the Red and the White Rose met for the first time in the struggle of battle.

The Lancastrians had the advantage of

L. of C.

position, and were so certain of victory that
Somerset issued orders that no quarter should be
given to the Yorkists, but the latter had firearms
of a rude description, which gave them a counter
advantage.   Clifford, however, kept them at bay
bravely, and prevented them from coming to close
conflict.   Meanwhile, Warwick, with his northern
warriors, entered the town from the other side,
and fell upon the King's troops with such vigour
that, as Hall says, "the King's army was profligate disposed, and all the chieftains of the field
almost slain and brought to confusion."   The
barriers were at length burst, and York entered
the town, and then in the streets were heard the
shouts of "A Warwick! a Warwick!" on the
other side "A York! a York!" and in the midst
the war cries of "King Henry! a Somerset! a
Percy! a Clifford!" etc., all intermingled with the
clash of swords upon armour and shield; the whir
of arrows flying through the air; the groans of
wounded and dying men, and the screams of flying
women; whilst the market-place was strewn with
the bodies of fallen men, and the streets flowed
with blood.   Shakspeare makes Clifford fall at
the hand of the Duke of York.   Warwick enters
crying—

" Clifford of Cumberland, 'tis Warwick calls!
And if thou do'st not hide thee from the bear
Now when the angry trumpet sounds alarm
And dead men's cries do fill the empty air,
Clifford, I say, come forth and fight with me!
Proud northern lord, Clifford of Cumberland,
Warwick is hoarse with calling thee to arms."

York, however, interposes, and claims the right of fighting with him.

" *Clifford.*—What seest thou in me, York? Why dost thou
       pause?
York.—With thy brave bearing I should be in love,
       But that thou art so fast mine enemy.
Clifford.—Nor should thy prowess want praise and esteem,
       But that 'tis shown ignobly and in treason.
York.—So let it help me now against thy sword,
       As I in justice and true right express it!
Clifford.—My soul and body on the action both!
York.—A dreadful lay!—address thee instantly.
       (They fight, and Clifford falls.)
Clifford.—La fin couronne les œuvres.   *(Dies.)*
York.—Thus war hath given thee peace, for thou art still.
       Peace with his soul, Heaven, if it be Thy will."

The slaughter of Lord Clifford at the hands of the Duke of York is the keynote to young Clifford's subsequent ruthless hatred of the House of York. Coming up to the body of his father, Shakspeare puts these words into his mouth—

" Wast thou ordain'd, dear father,
To lose thy youth in peace, and to achieve

" The silvery livery of advised age,
  And in thy reverence, and thy chair-days thus
  To die in ruffian battle?   Even at this sight
  My heart is turn'd to stone; and while 'tis mine
  It shall be stony.   York not our old men spares:
  No more will I their babes; tears virginal
  Shall be to me even as the dew to fire;
  And beauty, that the tyrant oft reclaims,
  Shall, to my flaming wrath, be oil and flax.
  Henceforth I will not have to do with pity
  Meet I an infant of the house of York,
  Into as many gobbets will I cut it
  As wild Medea young Absyrtus did.
  In cruelty will I seek out my fame.
  Come thou new ruin of old Clifford's house.
                              (Taking up the body.)
  As old Æneas did Anchises bear,
  So bear I thee upon my manly shoulders.
  But then Æneas bore a living load,
  Nothing so heavy as these woes of mine."

Although the Lancastrians fought bravely, nothing could withstand the superior number of the Yorkists, combined, as it was, with the military skill and impetuous valour of the Earl of Warwick, and in a short space of time there lay dead the Duke of Somerset and the Earls of Northumberland and Stafford; and the Duke of Buckingham and the Earl of Wiltshire and Ormond grievously wounded. Thus deprived of their chief leaders, the King being a mere cipher, the Lancastrians threw down their weapons and fled, Wentworth flinging down the Royal standard and spurring his horse in the direction of Suffolk. The poor King was captured; but York treated him with great courtesy and kindness, conducted him to St. Alban's Abbey, where they prayed together at the shrine of the martyr, and then went together, victor and vanquished, to London.

The Yorkists were now in the ascendant, but acted with great moderation. There were no executions and no attainders; so Clifford succeeded to the title and kept the estates. The King was again attacked by his old malady, and again was Richard of York appointed Protector; but Queen Margaret now began to exhibit her qualities, and to intrigue in politics. She was truly an able and brave woman, but vindictive and rash. She succeeded in ousting York from the Protectorship, and took measures for crushing him effectually; and again the flames of war broke out.

Lord Clifford did not, under these circumstances, sit at home brooding over his misfortunes and the bitterness of his hatred to the house of York. He was always on the alert, at London or elsewhere, attending on Councils of State or engaged in the field. He fought at Bloreheath, in 1459, and at Northampton, in 1460, on both of which occasions his party suffered a defeat; but Margaret, nothing daunted, raised an army of 18,000 men, and proceeded at their head into Yorkshire, in face of the frosts and snows of the December of 1460. The Duke of York, with a small army of 5,000 men, went from London and threw himself into Sandal Castle, by Wakefield, there to await the arrival of his son Edward, Earl of March, who was mustering forces in the Welsh Marches. The Queen came with her army upon Wakefield Green, with the Duke of Somerset, son of the slain Duke, in chief command, and Clifford and Wiltshire, son of the Earl who fell at St. Alban's, in command of ambuscades, one on each side. Then, aware of her numerical superiority, she appeared before Sandal, and summoned the Duke to come forth and fight her. "What, are you afraid of encountering an army led by a woman? Cowardly poltroon! can you be fit to wear the crown of England, who shut yourself up in a castle against a woman?" York called a council of war, and was earnestly dissuaded against running the hazard of a battle before the arrival of his son; but, taunted by the jeers of the Queen, he felt that his honour was concerned in fighting at once, despite the numerical odds, and forth he went with his small army, not one-third that of the Queen.

The Duke sallied forth and met Somerset, with a comparatively small force, on Wakefield Green, whom he attacked with great vigour, anticipating, with his better-disciplined men, an easy victory ; but the ambuscades under Clifford and Wiltshire came out upon his flanks, whilst a contingent of Northern Borderers attacked his rear, and thus, completely surrounded, his small force succumbed, the White Rose drooped, and the Red, for the first time, was triumphant. This battle brought to an end the ambitious aspirations of Richard of York. He was one of the first to fall, and with him Sir Thomas Neville, Lord Salisbury's son, and Lord Harrington, the husband of Katherine Neville, his daughter. Lord Salisbury himself was wounded, but not sufficiently to prevent his galloping off from the scene. Clifford however, followed in hot pursuit, captured, and sent him to Pontefract Castle, where he was at once beheaded.

Previously, however, to his pursuit of the father, Clifford was guilty of that dastardly act upon his son, the Earl of Rutland, which has stamped his name with infamy, and has given significance to his sobriquet of "Black-faced Clifford." The Duke of York had with him, in Sandal Castle, his family, including the youthful Earl of Rutland. Boy-like, he must needs go and see the battle, and nothing could dissuade him. " I will go," said he, " and see my father kill the cruel Queen; and when I am a man I will go and fight, and kill his enemies too." " A battle is not a place, Lord Edmund," replied his tutor and chaplain, Sir Robert Aspall, " for boys. A stray arrow might kill you." " Think not, sir priest," replied the brave boy, " that a son of Richard 'of York is afraid of an arrow! Stay under shelter of these walls, like craven priest, if you will; I shall go and see the deeds of men who are men !" Seeing that nothing could turn the boy from his purpose, his tutor resolved to go with him to keep him out of harm's way, nothing loth himself to witness the conflict of arms. When the battle was over, and the vanquished flying, Sir Robert led his charge away towards Sandal. They had not proceeded far, when they encountered a steel-clad warrior on horseback, with blood dropping from his sword. Perceiving from his apparel that he was a youth of distinction, the warrior dismounted, and, holding his horse by the reins, inquired who he was. "Then," as Hall says, "the young gentleman, dismayed, had not a word to speak, but kneeled on his knees, imploring mercy and desiring grace, both with holding up his hands and making dolorous countenance, for his speech was gone for fear. 'Save him,' said his chaplain, 'for he is a Prince's son, and peradventure may do you good hereafter.' With that word Lord Clifford marked him, and said, 'By God's blood! thy father slew mine, and so will I do to thee and all thy kin,' and with that word, struck the Earl to the heart with his dagger, and bade the chaplain bear the Earl's mother and brother word what he had done, and said, adding, 'By this act, Lord Clifford was accompted a tyrant and no gentleman.'"

Not satisfied with this cowardly act of vindictiveness, Lord Clifford resolved to carry his vengeful hatred on, by insulting the dead. He returned to the field, now strewn with corpses, sought for, and found that of the Duke of York, and cutting off his head, stuck it upon a lance and carried it, as the most acceptable trophy, to the tent of the Queen, who received it with ill-timed merriment and jest. She made a paper crown and placed it on the head, with an inscription—"This is he who would have been King of England," and gave directions for it to be conveyed, along with that of Salisbury, to York, and placed over one of the gates, adding, "Leave room for the head of my Lord of Warwick, for it shall soon bear them company!"

Queen Margaret, flushed with her victory, marched towards London, but met with the Earl of Warwick, in February, 1461, at St. Alban's, and there defeated him, after which the poor captive King was released and brought to his Queen in Lord Clifford's tent. But Edward, the quondam Earl of March, now Duke of York, had come up and joined Warwick, who, together, entered London and were welcomed by the citizens, who favoured the house of York. Margaret, fearing to meet their united forces, returned northward, her strongholds and most devoted friends being in the northern counties, especially on the Scottish borders, whither she was followed by Duke Edward. She had come to York, and lay there with 60,000 men, when she heard that York and Warwick had reached Pontefract with an army of 40,000 men. Anxious to prevent the passage of the Aire by the enemy, she moved to Towton, some eight miles off York, and there was fought the memorable and decisive battle which placed the crown on the head of Edward IV. The Lancastrians had seized Ferrybridge under Lord Fitzwalter, and Clifford, as courageous as he was cruel, undertook to dislodge him, which he accomplished. But Lord Falconbridge crossed the Aire three miles higher, at Castleford, and attacked Clifford in the flank with a superior force. Clifford fled towards the Queen's camp, and when he arrived at Dittingdale, two miles off Towton, feeling thirsty after his exertions, he removed his gorget and stooped to drink at a streamlet, when an arrow struck him in the throat, and the murderer of Rutland and insulter of the dead Richard of York fell to rise no more.

The Shepherd Lord.

OR ever memorable in the annals of England will be Palm Sunday in the year 1461, and equally so the little hamlet of Towton, by Tadcaster. There and then was fought, in a blinding snowstorm, what Camden calls "the English Pharsalia," the greatest battle hitherto fought on English soil, where Englishman met Englishman, and kinsman kinsman, in deadly conflict, and in which quarter was neither asked nor given. The conflict lasted ten hours, and the pursuit of the fugitives was continued until the middle of Monday. 60,000 Lancastrians were met by 40,000 Yorkists, and 36,000 corpses and dying men lay that Sunday night on the snow of the fields, roads, and hillsides, whilst the river and streamlets ran with torrents of blood, and the snow became encrimsoned as it fell. The fight inclined in favour of the Red Rose, under the command of the Duke of Somerset, although York and

Warwick performed prodigies of valour with their smaller forces, and the day must have gone against the White Rose, when, towards evening, the banner of the Mowbrays was seen approaching, and the Duke of Norfolk came up with a body of fresh troops, who made a vigorous attack on the Lancastrians, which at once turned the scale, and changed what seemed to be a defeat into a decisive victory, which was virtually the deposition of Henry VI., and the elevation of Edward IV. to the throne—a transference of the crown from the House of Lancaster to that of York.

The shades of evening were falling over the forest lands around Skipton, some week or ten days after the battle. The surrounding hills were covered with snow, and a fierce wind raged round the towers of the castle, whilst the boughs of the trees crashed against each other, and ever and anon a hugh branch, reft from the parent stem, was flung with fury to the earth.

Within the castle, in a room overlooking the courtyard, sat the Lady Clifford, with her young children, two or three female attendants, and the chaplain of the household. It was very unlike a

modern drawing-room, and, in these Sybarite
days, would be looked upon as a very comfortless
apartment; yet was it a fair specimen of the
drawing-room of the period. Instead of Ax-
minster or Aubusson carpets, the floors were
strewn with rushes; instead of oil paintings from
the hands of eminent masters, the walls were hung
with tapestries of Arras, more to cover the rough
nakedness of the stonework and exclude draughts
than for æsthetic purposes; the furniture of the
room consisted of a table, two or three chairs,
and a few stools of rough carpentry, not in
mahogany or rosewood, but of the native oak,
hewn out of the woodlands of the demesne. On
the hearthstone blazed a fire of wood, sputtering
as the sleet fell into it down the wide open
chimney. There was no grate, fender, or fire-
irons, but beside the hearth lay a heap of fresh
wood, to be thrown on the fire as required;
and when the embers required stirring, a
stick from the heap was used for that
purpose.

Lady Clifford sat in silence, brooding in
thought over her absent husband, with an
occasional heavy-drawn sigh; the children were
gambolling about the room in innocent uncon-

sciousness of the perils to which their father was
exposed ; the chaplain joined in their romps, and
amused them by telling them tales of Fairyland
and the good deeds of holy saints ; and the handmaidens were sitting apart, plying their distaffs
and spinning-wheels, and indulging in the usual
gossip of an isolated castle and the surrounding
village, but maintained it in an undertone,
so as not to disturb the meditations of their
lady.

"What a fearful night it is," said Lady
Clifford, as a terrific gust of wind came roaring
round the towers of the castle, seeming almost to
shake them to their foundations, stoutly as they
were built. "It is terrible even here, sitting as
we are under the protection of these strong
walls ; what must it be to those who are exposed
to its fury, camped, perchance, on some wild
moor, and surrounded by enemies ?"

At this moment a trumpet summons for
admittance to the castle was heard ; and presently
the seneschal entered the room, stating that
a knight was without the gate with tidings of
great importance.

"Who is he?" asked Lady Clifford. "Do you
know him ?"

I

"Yes, my lady, he is Sir John de Barnoldswick, who accompanied my lord, and I fear me he brings intelligence of evil import."

"Admit him instantly, and bring him hither."

The rattling of the chains of the drawbridge was heard, and the sound of opening the ponderous castle gates, followed by the tramping of a horse in the courtyard, and the heavy footsteps of a steel-clad warrior on the stone stairs, and a tall, martial-looking figure, but with melancholy gait and drooping head, entered the room and made a profound obeisance to the lady of the castle, but without speaking a word of salutation.

"Whence comest thou, Sir Knight, and what are thy tidings?" inquired Lady Clifford, in tremulous accents.

"I come from the field of battle, lady, and my tidings are evil."

"Let us hear them; I am a soldier's wife, and ought not to shrink from calamitous intelligence," she replied, although her nervous trembling belied her utterance.

"Know, then, lady, that a great and disastrous battle has been fought near Tadcaster, and the

Lancastrian cause lost. I fought till the last under the Clifford banner; saw many a brave fellow of the Vale of Craven fall around me, and barely escaped to bring the news hither."

" And what of the King and the brave Queen Margaret ? "

" Alas! I know not; they and the Prince of Wales were in York when the battle was fought. All I know is that Somerset and the King's troops were utterly defeated, and fled northward, with Warwick and the Duke of York in hot pursuit."

" And what of my lord ? Fled he too ? He would never turn his back to the foes of his King."

" He did not, lady; had he been present, the result might have been different. He was not in the engagement."

" What mean you by ' not in the engagement ' ? Surely he, of all men, would not stand aloof on such an occasion ? "

" Alas ! lady, I fear to tell you why."

" Speak, man! is he dead? or why was he absent ? "

" It is too true, lady, that he can no longer fight in defence of his King."

"Then he is dead!" cried Lady Clifford, in an agony of despair.

"He fell, my lady, on the eve of the battle, after a glorious act of valour, by a random shot. Heaven rest his soul!"

"Heaven help my poor children!" cried Lady Clifford, and fell to the floor in a swoon, the mother's instinctive love for her offspring prevailing over her grief for her own loss. And truly, she had reason to fear for them. Her husband, "Black-faced Clifford," as he was called, had an inveterate hatred for the House of York; he had murdered, in cold blood, the young Duke of Rutland, brother of Edward of York; had cut off the head of Richard, Duke of York; and had caused the Earl of Salisbury, father of Warwick, to be executed at Pontefract; and it was tolerably certain that York, the future King, and Warwick, his General, would seek to take vengeance on the children of him who had committed those atrocities.

The Dukes of York and Warwick marched triumphantly to York, and were submissively received by the authorities, and there they celebrated the festival of Easter with great splendour. Hastings, Stafford, and others had been made Knights-Bannerets on the field; Devon and Wilts were decapitated by martial law, and their heads placed on the bar gate of York, whence those of Richard of York and the Earl of Salisbury, the fathers of York and Warwick, had been removed; and, after settling affairs in the north, the victors marched to London, and were welcomed by the citizens with loud demonstrations of joy, the Londoners being staunch Yorkists.

Lady Clifford prepared to meet her untoward fate, and took measures for the safety of her children. Her old friend, the venerable Prior of Bolton, who had made himself acquainted with all that had taken place since the battle of Towton, so far as could be learnt in that remote spot, mounted his mule and rode over to the Castle. He was received courteously and with dutiful reverence by Lady Clifford, and, moreover, with joy, as she wished to consult him, above all others, as to her future line of conduct.

"I am at a loss, holy father, to think what I can do. I suppose there is no hope of retrieval on the part of Queen Margaret?"

"I am afraid not. The Queen is endeavouring

to raise another army in the north, but I fear with little chance of success."

"What, then, will be the effect upon the adherents of the House of Lancaster? I suppose executions, attainders, and confiscations?"

"Precisely so; and Lord Clifford, one of the most bitter foes of the House of York, will certainly be included in the first list, his title extinguished, and his estates confiscated."

"And my poor children will thus lose all their inheritance; but it is not that I dread this so much as the vengeance of the Duke—King now, I presume—and of the Earl of Warwick. I fear me that even if their lives are not sacrificed, they will be cast into dungeons, to languish out their lives."

"Your apprehensions, my daughter, are, unfortunately, but too well-founded, and we must consult on some measures for their safety. You need not fear molestation until Edward has seated himself securely on the throne, and will be safer within the walls of this castle than elsewhere. But it will be wise to make provision for removal to some secure retreat as soon as the Acts of Attainder have passed, and the

King begins to take vengeance on his foes, for then Skipton will pass into other hands."

" I bethink me of such a place," said Lady Clifford. " Your council is wise. I can go to the mansion of my father, Lord Vesci, on his Londesborough estates, near Market Weighton, where it will be possible to reside as far removed from the world as if out of the world. There I could bring up my children, without notice, until the cloud had passed over, or until a change in the wheel of fortune shall restore the House of Lancaster to the throne."

After some further discussion, the Prior saw that this was the best plan that could be adopted; and it was arranged that measures should be taken for departure at any moment, when there should be indications of the towers of Skipton becoming untenable, and, after a parting benediction, the reverend Prior mounted his mule, and returned home.

King Edward lost no time in taking steps to paralyse effectually any further efforts on the part of the adherents of the rival House. He called together a Parliament, and one of the first measures laid before it was an Act of Attainder against all the nobles and men of rank who had

appeared in arms against his legitimate claim to
the crown, which, now that he had been successful, was deemed treason.   The demesnes of John,
Lord Clifford, extended for seventy miles, with an
interval of ten, from Skipton into the heart of
Westmoreland, with four castles—those of
Brougham, Appleby, Brough, and Pendragon,
besides that of Skipton.   The Westmoreland
estates, with the tenure Baronies of Vipont and
Westmoreland, had been inherited by Robert de
Clifford, third baron, from his great-aunt,
Isabella, daughter and co-heiress of the last male
heir of the family of De Vipont.   By the Act of
Attainder all these fair lands and castles were
reft away from the family, the Barony of de
Clifford was declared to be extinct for ever, and
all the estates, forests, moors, castles, tenements,
mills, and goods escheated to the Crown.   In the
fourth of the reign, the castle, manor, and lordship of Skipton, and the manor of Morton were
granted in tail male to Sir Edward Stanley,
but in the fifteenth year were transferred to
the King's brother, Richard, Duke of Gloucester,
to hold till death.

It is proverbial that bad news flies rapidly, and
it was not long ere news arrived at Skipton and

Bolton of the Act of Attainder. The Prior had come over to the castle to advise with Lady Clifford. "You must take your departure at once," said he. "The agents of the usurper will be here anon and take possession in the name of the King, and it is not at all improbable that they will have instructions to remove your children from your care, and immure them in some place of captivity, if nothing worse befalls them, as the offspring of one of the most determined enemies of the House of York."

"I have sent a confidential servant," she replied, "to Lord Vesci, my father, who sends word back that preparation shall be made for my reception at Londesborough."

"Nothing remains, then," said the Prior, "but to secure your jewels and other portable articles of value, with such of the family papers as you may deem it wise to preserve, and to set off on your journey, with an escort sufficient for your protection, but not so large as to attract undue notice."

Lady Clifford had left the castle in charge of the seneschal, to deliver it into the King's hands, and rode forth on a palfrey, disguised as a farmer's wife. She was accompanied by three or four horsemen in similar disguise, with whom the children rode, and was followed at some distance by some half-dozen servitors clad as peasants, but bearing concealed weapons for the purpose of defence, if needful, as it was probable that they might meet with disbanded soldiers, who might not be over scrupulous in waylaying and robbing chance travellers. The party, as far as possible, went along by-ways, so as to escape observation, but these were sometimes so rough as to compel them to take the more beaten high roads, and, passing by Otley, Tadcaster, and York, arrived at Londesborough without any mishap or adventure of consequence.

Londesborough is supposed to have been the Delgovitia of the Romans, and was seated at the foot of the road from Eboracum, one branch going to the ferry over the Humber at Brough, and the other across Holderness to the seaport at Ravenspurn. It is presumed, also, that the Saxon king, Eadwine, had a palace here, and that within its walls he held his conference with Paulinus, which resulted in the demolition of the temple of Woden at Goodmandingham, two miles distant. The De Vescis had built a mansion here, and laid out a park with a noble avenue of trees, a mile in length, in which Lady Clifford had played when a child, Londesborough having been her birthplace. The estates passed at the death of Henry de Bromflete, in 1466, to his daughter, Margaret, and through her to the De Cliffords, in whose possession they remained until the death, without issue male, of Henry V., and last Earl of Cumberland, when they passed, by the marriage of his daughter and heiress, to the Earl of Burlington, of the Boyle family. The old mansion was taken down in 1819, and the park divided into farms.

It was with a feeling of melancholy satisfaction that Lady Clifford found herself in a species of security in her ancestral home, and she longed to ramble at will about the park and village, as she had been wont to do in bygone days, but it was not prudent to indulge in such pleasures, her position necessitating the utmost seclusion of herself and children from the outer world. About a month afterwards she sent a messenger secretly to Skipton, to ascertain what had occurred there since she left, and on his return learnt that the King's Commissioners had visited the Castle and taken possession of it and the estates in the name of the Crown; moreover, that they had made particular inquiries after Lady Clifford and " the brats of the Butcher of Wake- field," but were put off by being told by the domestics in charge that they had left Skipton a month ago, and gone they knew not where, but believed to some country across the sea. The Yorkists, however, seem to have suspected that this was not the truth, and shortly afterwards strangers of sinister aspect were observed to be lurking about Londesborough. This excited great terror in the breast of Lady Clifford, who saw clearly that her children were in great danger, and she took prompt measures for their safety. She had three children—Henry, the eldest, about seven years of age; Richard, the younger son; and a daughter—Elizabeth, affianced to one of the Plumptons of Plumpton. She soon decided on her plans. The maid who had nursed her when a child, had married a shepherd on the estate, and Henry was placed under her charge, to be brought up as her child, to live as his foster-parents lived, and follow the occupation of tending sheep on the hillsides, in which measure, he, being an intelligent child, cheerfully acquiesced, assumed the shepherd's garb, and attended to the duties of his new

station without the slightest murmur, his sole
regret being the enforced absence from his
mother. Richard was sent in charge of a
careful servant to Ravenspurn, and thence
carried across the sea to Flanders, whilst
Elizabeth, who, it was supposed, would not
be molested, remained as the sole comfort and
solace of her mother. These measures were not
taken a moment too soon, for " a little after they
were thus disposed of, the adverse party examined
their mother about them, who told them that
she had ordered them to be carried beyond sea to
be bred up there; but whether they were alive
or not she could not tell, which answer satisfied
them for the present," and, after making strict
search without effect, they departed.

In 1466, Lord de Vesci died, and Lady
Clifford, as his heiress, succeeded to his estates,
when a rumour reached Londesborough from the
Court that the King suspected that the children
were in concealment there, upon which Lady
Clifford sent the shepherd, with his wife and
young Henry, to a farm in a remote and wild
part of Cumberland, where there were few
inhabitants, and no roads upon which passengers
would travel, excepting from one sheep track to

another. In this lonely solitude, tending his
sheep on the bleak hills, Henry grew up from
boyhood to youth, and from youth to manhood—
a mere shepherd and little more. His fare was
that of an ordinary peasant—oaten or rye bread,
occasionally swine flesh, and water from the
running brook. His bed consisted of sheepskins
on a heap of straw, and his shelter from the in-
clemency of the weather a straw-thatched cottage.
He associated with the few scattered people
of the district as one of themselves, and joined
the young men in the rude sports of the period.
He grew up without any education whatever,
and knew neither how to read nor write; yet
he had a soul attuned to higher things, and when
abroad at night with his sheep would observe
the constellations in the heavens, and weave
theories in his own mind relative to the origin,
motions, and uses of the glittering specks which
studded the firmament over his head, a study
which he afterwards pursued with more intelligence, in company with the Canons of
Bolton at Barden Tower. Thus he lived until
his thirty-second year, thinking only to live and
die a Cumberland shepherd, and possibly to
marry, and be the progenitor of a race of

peasants, who should have no reminiscences of the glories of Skipton, or the martial deeds of their illustrious ancestors.

The political world of England, however, had not stood still in the interval, mighty events had been taking place. Edward, the King, had been gathered to his fathers, after the judicial murder of his brother, the Duke of Clarence. His sons, Edward V. and the Duke of York, were murdered by their uncle, Richard of Gloucester, who usurped the throne. Henry, Earl of Richmond, with Lancastrian blood in his veins, invaded England, and the battle of Bosworth was fought in the year 1485, when the usurper Richard was slain, and Richmond ascended the throne as King Henry VII.

The Yorkist dynasty having now come to an end, there remained no more fear for the Cliffords. The shepherd was brought from the fells of Cumberland to Londesborough. Soon after the Attainder was reversed, the confiscated estates restored, and the Clifford banner again floated in the breeze from the towers of Skipton. But the Shepherd Lord felt not at home amid the splendours of his castle, and he fitted up one of the keeper's lodges in Barden Forest for his residence, where he lived in great simplicity, spending his days in hunting and his nights in watching the stars, and studying astronomy with the Canons of Bolton, with such rude instruments as were then to be procured.

In 1513, when about sixty years of age, he received a summons to attend the expedition into Scotland, with a contingent of men-at-arms, and held a command at the battle of Flodden, where he displayed the hereditary military skill and valour of the Cliffords.

> "From Penigent to Pendle Hill,
>   From Linton to Long Addingham,
> And all that Craven coasts did till,
>   They with the lusty Clifford came.
> All Staincliffe Hundred went with him,
>   With striplings strong from Wharfedale,
> And all that Hauton Hills did climb,
>   With Longstroth eke and Litton dale,
> Whose milk-fed fellows, fleshly bred,
>   Well brown'd, with sounding bows upbend,
> All such as Horton fells had fed,
>   On Clifford's banners did attend."
>   —*Ballad of Flodden Field.*

He survived the battle ten years, died in 1523, at about the seventieth year of his age, and was buried with his ancestors in the church of Bolton.

Margaret, Lady Clifford, married for her second husband, Launcelot Threlkeld, and bore him three daughters. She survived her first husband thirty years, and the restitution seven years, dying in 1491, at Londesborough. She was buried in the church there, near the altar, under a slab, with an inlaid brass plate bearing the following inscription :—"Orate pro anima Margarete, D'ne Clifford et Vescy, olim spouse nobilissimi viri joh'is D'm Clifford et Westmoreland, filie et hereditis Henrici Bromflet, quondam D'ni Vescy, etc. . . . Matris Henrici Domini Clifford, Westmoreland et Vescy, quae obiit 15 die mens Aprilis, Anno Domini 1491, cujus corpus sub hoc marmore est humatum."

K

The Felons of Ilkley.

HE town of Ilkley, on the Wharfe, now so well known to tourists for the beauty of its situation and the grandeur of the natural scenery surrounding it, and to invalids for the invigorating and restorative qualities of its waters, is a place of very ancient date. It was built and fortified by the proprætor, Virius Lupus, in the time of the Emperor Severus, the fortress being situated on a precipitous bank of the Wharfe, and a cohort stationed there. Remains of the intrenchments are still to be seen, and altars, sepulchral stones, and other memorials of the Roman Olicaria have frequently been disinterred. Under the Saxons, too, it was a place of some importance, with a church and priest. In the churchyard there are some remarkable relics of this age, consisting of three stone crosses, with curiously convoluted knots and scroll work. Afterwards it sank into a mere village, but with a

grammar school, founded in 1601 by the parish-
ioners, and so remained until recent times,
when the fame of its salubrious springs went
forth over the land and attracted crowds of
fashionable invalids and hypochondriacs.

It was in the latter half of the seventeenth
century, when the reign of the Puritans had
come to an end, and the "Merry Monarch" had
been restored to the throne of the Stuarts, bringing with him the profligate, licentious, and pro-
fane manners of the Court of Versailles, that one
fine summer's afternoon a party of roysterers,
who had been at a cock-fight, burst into the
kitchen of the mud-built and thatched alehouse
of Ilkley, calling upon Mistress Laycock, the ale-
wife, for sundry flagons of ale wherewith to
moisten their throats, parched and dry with
halloaing and shouting out bets at the cocking
match. The twenty years' rule of the Puritans,
with the suppression of sports, theatres, and
other amusements, and the substitution of long
sermons and long prayers, had produced the
natural reaction, and now the people of Ilkley,
as in other places, returned with renewed zest
to their bull-baiting, dog fights, cudgel matches,
and their more innocent amusements of dancing

round the maypole, holding yule-feasts and
village fairs, and mumming in grotesque masquer-
ade on Plough Monday.

The roysterers who thus boisterously invaded
Dame Laycock's kitchen were Tom Heber, a
young scapegrace, son of Reginald Heber, a
barrister-at-law of the Middle Temple, and an
offshoot of the ancient family of Heebeare, who
had been settled in Craven for some centuries.
He had been brought up in the old gabled
and cross-timbered house of his father in Ilkley,
had been well educated, and was a clever and
accomplished young fellow ; moreover, his father
had taken him once or twice to London, and
he had been a witness of the revels and
immoralities of Whitehall, which struck his
fancy as being the perfection of human bliss.
His companions this afternoon were Will
Hudson, the village cobbler, who infinitely pre-
ferred swaggering at a bull-baiting to hammering
at the lapstone ; Walter Pollard, a shoeing
smith, whose feats at tossing off the contents of a
blackjack were the admiration of his comrades ;
Jack Smithers, a journeyman flesher, whose dog
was the pride of the village for his pluck in
tackling any animal of his size or more than his

size; and two or three other rapscallions of the village, who were ever foremost in a brawl, and more frequently seen in the purlieus of the ale-house than in pursuit of their proper vocations.

These worthies had now seated themselves on the long-settle which faced a fire of wood on the hearth-stone, over which swung a large cauldron, and called out vociferously for the ale. " Now then, Mother Laycock," shouted Heber, " when is this ale coming ? " " The old score's not paid yet, Master Thomas," replied she, from another room, " and I told you that I would not draw another pint until that was paid." " Oh! you won't, won't you; then your crockery shall suffer for your obstinacy; so here goes," and down he dashed an earthenware jug on the floor, upon which she rushed in, and opening a cupboard door, showed a long score chalked against him. " Oh! hang the score," said he, " you know I shall pay you some day; my father cannot be so hard as to keep me entirely without money." " But, Master Thomas, I cannot afford to give such long trust." " Now, Mistress Laycock, you know I am a good customer, and always pay in the long run; is this ale forthcoming ? " and down he threw

another piece of crockery, adding, " It shall all
go if you do not bring the ale." The old dame,
terrified at the breakage of her pots, then gave
in and produced the ale, adding it to the score on
the cupboard door.

The ale jug passed merrily round, and the conversation turned first upon the points of the cock-
fight they had been witnessing, and then upon
the merits of the competitors in a wrestling
match which was coming off the following
Sunday. They then began to complain of their
scant fortunes, not attributing it at all to their
lack of industry in business. " I'll tell you what
it is," said Heber, " its a parlous shame that my
father keeps me so short of money." " It is ! it
is !" echoed his companions. " He has brought me
up as a gentleman, and given me a good education,
but does not allow me the means to support that
position, and I say again that it is cursed shame ;
but never mind, boys, the time is coming when I
shall have plenty of gold to scatter about amongst
you, my jolly companions." " Brayvo ! brayvo !
three cheers for Squire Heber." " Meanwhile,"
continued he, " it is the best philosophy to make
the best of what we have, to enjoy life as much
as we can, to dance, and drink, and sing,

and fling dull care to the winds. So drink, boys! drink! and I will sing you one of Cowley's new songs which I picked up in London." And he trolled forth—

"Fill the bowl with rosy wine ;
Around our temples roses twine ;
And let us cheerfully awhile,
Like the vine and roses smile,
Crown'd with roses we contemn
Gyges' wealthy diadem.

To-day is ours ; what do we fear ?
To-day is ours ; we have it here.
Let's treat it kindly, that it may
Wish, at least, with us to stay.
Let's banish business ; banish sorrow ;
To the gods belongs to morrow."

Of course, the song was rapturously applauded by the listeners, who caught the general senti- ment, but were unable to understand the allusions or appreciate the refinement of the language. Suddenly Heber exclaimed—"Lads! a bright thought has flashed across my mind. We want money, and money we must have. Old Alic Squire is well to do, and always has a consider- able sum of money by him, and it would be a charity to relieve him of the care and anxiety of keeping it in that lonely house of his. The thing could be easily done. We have but to disguise

ourselves, break into his house, take what we
require, and leave him to attribute the appropria-
tion, I won't call it theft, to professional
burglars." The confederates highly approved of
the scheme, and gave a ready assent, after which
they arranged a plan of operation, and agreed to
carry it into execution three nights hence.

On the appointed evening they assembled
at the house of Will, the cobbler, where they
donned sundry disguises, armed themselves with
cudgels, an axe, a crowbar, and a wooden wedge,
and sallied forth into the moonlight. Squire's
farmhouse lay at a little distance from the village,
shrouded in trees. It was occupied by himself,
a widower, and his married daughter, Elizabeth
Beecroft; whilst in the barn, on that night, slept
one Jane Beanland. The moon was nearly at
full, but masses of clouds drifted across its face,
obscuring its beams, so that it only shone out at
intervals. As they approached the house at
midnight a profound silence prevailed; not a dog
barked, and it was only broken occasionally by
the distant hooting of an owl. A minute or two
were only required to force open the door by the
application of the wedge and three or four blows
of the axe, and Heber, Hudson, and Pollard

entered the house, the others remaining outside. The old man had been awakened by the noise of forcing the door open, and he came from his bedroom half-dressed, demanding what they wanted by thus breaking into his house. " Money," was the reply, " and if you do not give it up we shall take it." " I have got no money for you," he answered, and, seizing upon a poker, he stood upon his defence, but was overpowered by a blow on the head, and the robbers then prized open his desk, but found in it not more than fifty shillings, and broke open a cupboard, taking from it a piece of beef, after which they went away, much disappointed at the smallness of their booty. Notwithstanding their disguise, they had been identified, Squire, in his deposition, stating that he recognised Tom Heber by his stature and the softness of his hand, which he felt when struggling with him ; Elizabeth, his daughter, whose room they had entered and "nearly smothered her in the bed clothes," also recognised " Mr. Thos. Heber," as one of the party ; and Jane Beanland deposed that, as she lay in the barn, she heard the voices of Mr. Thos. Heber, of Holling, and William Hudson, of Ilkley, when they were breaking open the door. Moreover,

Elizabeth Longfellow gave evidence that going into the alehouse of Josias Laycock, where Walter Pollard was drinking, she overheard him say, " I am now making Bess Squire's half-crowns fly." They had left behind them also an iron gavelock, a staff, and a wedge, which were identified as having been in their possession a day or two before the crime was committed.

These facts having come to light, warrants were issued for the apprehension of the offenders, and they were brought before Walter Hawkes-worth, of Hawkesworth, the nearest magistrate. This gentlemen was a friend of Serjeant Heber, and, knowing Tom well, he expressed his regret at seeing him placed in that situation, who, however, laughingly replied that it was only done for a lark, but the magistrate, after hearing the depositions, with a grave countenance, said " It might be a lark, but at the same time it was a felony, and a serious outrage of the law, and he had no alternative but to commit them to York for trial at the assizes."

They were consequently arraigned at the assizes on a charge of burglary, but escaped the usual severe punishment, partly on the ground that the crime was committed as a frolic, which was the line of defence, partly through family influence, and partly through the powerful agency of money.

It is a remarkable fact that there were then resident in Ilkley two families—the Hebers, of whom was the criminal, and the Longfellows, a member of whom was a witness on the trial against him, and that from them are descended two of the most charming poets of modern times—Reginald Heber, Bishop of Calcutta, author of " Palestine," and Henry Wadsworth Longfellow, whose writings are as much admired in England as in his native America.

The Ingilby Boar's Head.

THE crest of the Ingilbys of Ripley is "A boar's head couped and erect arg., tusked or," which was obtained by an early knight of the family, in a romantic fashion, and as the reward for a valiant achievement.

In the reign of Edward the Confessor the manor of Ripley was held by Merlesweyn, a powerful Danish lord, and owner of many another manor and estate in the same district. He joined in the Gospatric insurrection against William the Conqueror, in favour of Edgar the Atheling, for which rebellion his lands were confiscated, and granted to Ralph de Paganel, a Norman noble who had fought at Hastings, and who besides became Lord of Leeds, Headingley, and extensive estates on the Ouse, the Aire, and the Nidd; holding the Merlesweyn estates *in capite* from the King; Leeds, etc., by the service of a knight's fee and a half, under the

Lacies of Pontefract; whilst lands at Adel, Arthington, etc., devolved on him in right of his wife, Matilda, daughter of Richard de Surdeval. He was the founder of the Priory of the Holy Trinity, York, upon which, in 1080, he bestowed the churches of Leeds and Adel.

From the Paganels, Ripley passed to the Trusbut family, how does not appear, and from them, by the marriage of the heiress, to the family of de Ros of Ingmanthorpe, a branch of the de Ros's of Hamlake and Holderness, who became the superior lords, under whom the manor was held for half a knight's fee, early in the twelfth century, by a family whose previous name is not recorded, but who adopted that of de Ripley from their possessions. From this family descended the famous Canon of Bridlington, Sir George de Ripley, in the fifteenth century, the alcnymist and "discoverer" of the philosopher's stone, as he professed, in 1470, and who contributed annually vast sums of money to the Knights of Rhodes for maintaining their warfare against the Mussulmans.

The Ingilbys are of Scandinavian origin, seated for a long period at Engelby, in Lincolnshire, whence they derived their surname, who, at the time of Domesday Book held three manors in Lincolnshire, two in the North Riding of Yorkshire, under the Bishop of Durham and William of Poictou, and one in Derbyshire. In 1350, or thereabouts, Sir Thomas de Ingilby, Justice of the Common Pleas, married Catherine or Luerne, daughter and heiress of Bernard (?) de Ripley, and came into possession of the Ripley estates, where he settled, and, seven years afterwards, obtained a charter for an annual fair and weekly market at Ripley.

The Ingilbys, still extant, have held a distinguished place among the families of Yorkshire, and many members of the family have been entrusted with high offices in Church and State, and become eminent in the field.

John Ingilby (*temp.* Richard II.), was the second founder of and benefactor to the Carthusan Monastery of Mount Grace, in Cleveland. John, born at Ripley in 1434, "did wondrously flourish in the reign of Henry VI." Sir William, his son, was knighted by "Lord Gloucester on Milton Field, in Holland, in 1482," for valour. A John de Ingilby was Prior of Sheen and Bishop of Llandaff, 1496-1500. Sir William, born 1515, was High Sheriff of Yorkshire and

Treasurer of Berwick, *temp.* Elizabeth. David, his second son, married Anne Nevile, daughter of Charles, sixth Earl of Westmoreland, by which marriage his representatives, with those of Nicholas Pudsey, are co-heirs of the abeyant Barony of Nevile of Raby. Francis, third son of Sir William, was a Roman Catholic priest, and was executed at York, in 1586, for performing the functions of his office in the realm. John, fifth son of Sir William, was presented in the list of recusants in 1604. William, eldest son of Sampson of Spofforth, fourth son of Sir William, was created baronet in 1642, and fought on the King's side at Marston Moor. His castle at Ripley was garrisoned for the King, and Cromwell, after the battle of Marston Moor, passing through Ripley, demanded lodgings for the night, which was at first refused by Lady Ingilby, but he was, after a parley, admitted, on the promise that his followers should not be guilty of any impropriety. She received him with a couple of pistols stuck in her apron string, and on leaving in the morning, he inquired the meaning of the two weapons. " I'll tell you," she replied, " why I had two ; it was that the second might be ready in case the first missed fire, for if you had be-

haved otherwise than peaceably I should have pis-
tolled you without the least remorse." Sir
William rebuilt Ripley Castle. In one of the
towers is the following inscription :—"In the
yiere of owre Ld. M.D.L.V. was this towre
buyldyd by Sir Willyam Ingilby, Knight;
Philip and Mary reigning that time." In the
great staircase window is a series of escutcheons
on stained glass, containing the arms of Ingilby
and of the families with whom they had inter-
married. Sir William, the second baronet, purchased the manor of Armley from the Mauliverers.
Sir John, the fourth baronet died 1772, when the
baronetcy expired. The baronetcy was revived
in 1781, in the person of John Ingilby, an illegitimate son of the fourth baronet of the previous
creation. Sir William Amcotts, his fourth son,
succeeded to the baronetcy of his maternal grandfather, Sir Wharton Amcotts, by special remainder, and to that of his father in 1815, but died
s.p., in 1854, when the baronetcy expired.

In 1866 the baronetcy was again restored, in
the person of the Rev. Henry John, nephew
of the above Sir John, in his succession by will to
the Ripley estates, whose son, Sir Henry Day is
the present holder, with (according to the new

Domesday Book, of 1876) an acreage in the West Riding of 10,000, producing a rental of £11,149 per annum.

In Ripley Castle there is, or was, a full-length portrait of a knight of the Ingilby family, attired in the hunting costume of the Plantagenet times, with the head of a wild boar at his feet. This is the presentment of Sir William Ingilby, a doughty warrior and a hunter of renown, who lived in the troublous reign of Edward II. Although the representative of the family still lived in Lincolnshire, not having yet acquired the Ripley estates, this Sir William resided on one of the Yorkshire estates not far distant from Ripley, and would be on terms of intimacy with the family of de Ripley, whose heiress was won by Sir Thomas Ingilby, the Justice of the Common Pleas, and who possibly might have been the son of Sir William. Sir William had gained some renown in the Scottish wars of King Edward I. against William Wallace, and had been an ardent and loyal supporter of the weak and unfortunate second Edward on his accession to the throne, from the fact of his being the son of the great and glorious King, the first of that name.

L

He remained loyal until the King gave himself up into the hands of his favourite, Piers Gaveston, who humoured his naturally depraved inclinations, and led him into acts of mal-government, which estranged the hearts of the people. He loaded him with benefits, bestowing on him great estates and much treasure. Amongst other grants he gave him the Lordship of Knaresborough Castle and forest, with divers liberties, franchises, and privileges, which led him to assume a high and dictatorial tone to the nobles of the realm, who expostulated with the King, and compelled him to banish the insolent foreigner. But the King, not able to learn wisdom in the school of experience, recalled him and bestowed fresh benefits upon him, which so exasperated the Barons that they rose in arms, with Thomas, Earl of Lancaster, at their head, captured the favourite in Scarborough Castle, and beheaded him. The King then took the Spensers into his favour, who became more intolerably oppressive than their predecessor, upon which the Barons again rose in arms, but were defeated in a battle at Boroughbridge, and nearly a hundred barons, knights, and other prisoners put to death, the Earl of Lancaster being beheaded at Pontefract. In the sequel, however, the Spensers met the same fate as Gaveston, the elder being executed at Bristol, and the younger at Hereford.

Notwithstanding his personal loyalty, Sir William became so disgusted at the imbecile conduct of the King, and the arrogance of his favourites, that he took up arms with the Barons for the purpose of removing them from the Royal councils. A bloody revenge was taken by the King on the leaders and more prominent members of the conspiracy, but those of lesser degree were permitted to escape capital punishment, being punished by fines, confiscations, etc., and lay under a cloud of disgrace until the barbarous murder of the King in Berkley Castle, and the accession of Edward III., removed the stigma.

In this latter category was included Sir William Ingilby, who would most probably have remained alienated from the good graces of the King had not a fortunate circumstance occurred, which restored him to favour, and which had an influence in enhancing the dignity of the family.

Sir William's residence was in the valley of the Nidd, "one of the most romantic, picturesque, and wealthy vales in England." Spreading around for a distance of several miles lay the magnificent Forest of Knaresborough, the home of wild cattle, wolves, wild boars, the roebuck, and other ferocious animals of the chase. To the east stood, on its craggy and almost inaccessible rock, overhanging the Nidd and the then small village of Knaresborough, the formidable fortress of Serlo de Burgh, whilst on the verge of the forest stood the splendid monastic establishments of Fountains, Bolton, Ripon, and other lesser houses. The forest has the reputation of having been one of the haunts of Robin Hood, one portion bearing traditionally the name of "Robin Hood's Park," whence he issued to pay his visits to the Abbey of Fountains, as recorded in ballad lore. In the western portion of the forest lay the Royal chase of Haverah Park (Hey-wra, the park of the wra or roe), consisting of 2,000 acres, densely wooded, and inhabited by beasts of chase, which were kept together and preserved by an oak paling, which encircled the park. The road thither from Knaresborough ran through the forest south of the Nidd, and across an upland, since famous for its chalybeate springs, and where there were then a few scattered

cottages, forming a small hamlet, which came to
be designated Heynragate—the road to Heynra
Park—which has since been corrupted into
Harrogate, and has become one of the most
fashionable inland watering places in the
kingdom.

The Castle and forest of Knaresborough
were granted to Serlo de Burgh, who built the
castle, after whom they were alternately in
the hands of the · Crown, or of some Royal
favourite on whom they had been bestowed.
Edward II. made a grant of them to Piers
Gaveston, on whose death they reverted to the
Crown. It was during this period that the King
came to Knaresborough Castle to relax himself
from the cares and anxieties of Royalty, by three
or four days' hunting in Haverah Park. He was
not attended by a large retinue, being only
accompanied by three or four friends, and a few
body servants ; huntsmen, beaters, and other
attendants of the chase being permanently
retained there, as well as hounds and all the
requisite hunting gear and weapons ; this was
because of his unpopularity with the people,
on account of his governing the realm upon the
advice of unworthy favourites. Hence he came

down with some degree of secrecy, in a species of incognito, and it was not known generally to the residents of the valley who the hunter was, the supposition being that he was some friend of the King's, who had been given permission to hunt in Haverah chase.

The day following his arrival at Knaresborough, the King rode through the forest to Haverah, accompanied by his friends, and a following of attendants bearing bows and arrows, boar spears, beating staves, and other implements of hunting, who were on foot. On entering the enclosures the attendants sent their dogs amongst the underwood and commenced beating the bushes, with loud cries to start the game. As these were very plentiful, a number of small animals, badgers, foxes, polecats, etc., were roused from their lairs in quick succession, and afforded considerable sport. Two or three stags were also started, one of which was killed by the King, by an arrow shot; and a wolf made his appearance, who displayed great pugnacity, and caused great excitement amongst the hunters. Towards noon the King and his friends sat down to a refection under the shadow of a patriarchal oak, which, from its size and evident age, rendered it possible

that it might have witnessed the Druidical
mysteries of the Brigantes. Again the beaters
and dogs commenced their operations, and were
rewarded by the appearance of a huge wild boar,
armed with a formidable pair of tusks, who rushed
into the glade where the hunters were assembled.
The dogs rushed upon him, barking with eager-
ness, and the King and his friends, taking boar
spears from the attendants, rode at a gallop
towards the animal, who gazed upon them for a
few moments, as if to measure the strength of his
opponents, and then turned and dashed amongst
the underwood, followed by the hounds and the
hunters.

Two or three of the dogs, venturing too
near the boar, were instantly ripped up, and the
hunters followed as best they might through the
tangled brushwood. The King, who was better
mounted than his friends, soon left them behind,
and, brandishing his spear, followed in the track
made by the boar, not without sundry scratches
from the projecting branches of the forest trees;
but the boar still kept ahead, occasionally turning
to look at the hounds who were yelping at his
heels, and then dashing onward again; whilst the
King, mounted on a powerful and fleet horse,

gradually gained on the beast, despite the obstacles that beset his path.

Although the forest of Knaresborough was a Royal appanage, the foresters, as the inhabitants of the district were called, possessed certain privileges of hunting therein, with certain limits ; from Haverah Park alone were they excluded, that domain being reserved exclusively for the King and those to whom he gave permission to hunt in the enclosure. Sir William Ingleby being a "forester," therefore had the right of following game in the forest outside the palings of Haverah. On the same day that the King went to hunt in Haverah Park, Sir William went out, boar spear in hand, in search of sport. He was not accompanied by either attendant or dog, trusting alone to his own natural prowess, in case he should meet with game. In his wanderings he had come near the palings of the park, and sat down to partake of a luncheon he had brought with him in his pocket. He was just finishing his meal when he heard the cry of hunting dogs, and immediately afterwards a crashing sound. Looking up he saw the palings give way, and a huge boar rushing through the gap, followed by half a dozen dogs and a man on horseback. He had just time to observe that the hunter was clad in a buff jerkin, with high-reaching boots, and was brandishing a boar spear and encouraging the hounds, when the boar, finding himself so hotly pursued, turned at bay, drove his tusks into a couple of the dogs, and then sprang upon the hunter, over-turning the horse, and laying the hunter prostrate on the sward. He was just on the point of dashing his tusks into the body of the fallen enemy, when Sir William rushed up, and with well directed aim struck his spear into the heart of the boar, which fell lifeless at his feet, and then, taking his knife from his girdle, with a huntsman's skill severed the head from the body, the whole occupying but a few minutes.

"And who are you, my brave fellow?" inquired the fallen hunter, whom Sir William had assisted in rising and disentangling from his horse.

"I am a denizen of the forest," replied Sir William. "As to my name, it matters not; but right glad am I to have been the means of rescuing you from the fangs of that monster."

"You have saved me from death, whoever you may be," said the hunter, "and your guerdon shall be equivalent to the service you have rendered me."

"May I be allowed to ask who you may be," continued Sir William, "who are hunting in the King's chase?"

"I am connected with the court of the King, who has come hither for the divertisement of hunting."

"The King, whom Heaven preserve, then is present in the chase?" inquired Sir William.

"He is," replied the hunter, "the remainder of the party will be here anon."

"How shall I know the King, for I shall wish to pay due respect to him?"

"Oh, he may be easily recognised, for he will remain covered, while all the rest momentarily remove their hats."

At this moment the rest of the hunting group came up, all of whom uncovered their heads.

"Now, do you recognise the king?" inquired the hunter,

"I do," he replied, dropping on his knee, "and crave pardon for the boldness of my language."

The King, for he it was, then told his followers how Sir William had saved his life, and that although he had declined giving his name, he would find that out, and would reward him suitably for so important a service.

"Please your Majesty," said one of the beaters, "I know who the gentleman is; he is Sir William Ingleby of Nidderdale."

"Sir William Ingleby?" said the King. "If I remember aright, you were one of those who, along with our kinsman, Lancaster, appeared in arms against our Royal authority."

"Not my Liege," replied Ingleby, "against your Royal authority, but against your evil advisers."

"Well," continued the King, with a slight scowl, "let bygones be bygones; you have done me a service which obliterates all that. You are from this moment restored to favour; in memory of what you have done this day, I decree that, for the future and all time, you and your family shall bear, as the crest of your arms, a boar's head. Let me see you shortly at my Court, and then I will see what further I can do out of gratitude for the service you have rendered me."

Sir William made a profound obeisance to the King, and from that time the fortunes of the Inglebys, from that circumstance, coupled with the fortunate marriage with the heiress of Ripley, continued to rise.

The Rev. Thomas Parkinson, in his " Lays and Leaves of the Forest" (1882), writes— " It is impossible to fix any date at which the various wild animals ceased to inhabit the forest. The wild cattle are not mentioned after the thirteenth century. Wolves were probably extinct in the fourteenth ; indeed there are traditions of their existence three centuries later. Deer there were in 1654 A.D., for William Fleetwood, Sergeant of the Duchy of Lancaster, was plaintiff in a suit against Ellis Markham for destruction of some deer, game, and trees in Haverah or Heywra Park, at that date. The last wild boar is said to have been slain in the Boar-hole in Haverah Park, in the reign of Charles II. By the middle of the reign of Elizabeth, however, say 1580 A.D., probably all, except very rare specimens indeed, the larger wild animals were gone. . . . Nominally, the district remained a Royal forest up to the time of its enclosure, under Act of Parliament, in 1771 A.D., but long before that date it had practically ceased to be a refuge for wild beasts, or to be used for the chase. As we have seen, its larger animals were extinct, and, besides losing its chief fauna, it has been denuded, in a great measure, of its green woods and forest monarchs. This is said to have been brought about chiefly by the existence of smelting furnaces for lead and iron in the neighbourhood."

The Eland Tragedy.

IN the reign of King Edward III., four gentlemen, the heads of four reputable county families, resided in their respective halls, within a short distance of each other, in the neighbourhood of Huddersfield. They were Sir John Eland, of Eland Hall; Sir Robert Beaumont, of Crosland Hall; Sir Hugh Quarmby, of Quarmby; and John Lockwood, of Lockwood. The family of Sir John Eland had been seated here for several generations, descended from Leisingus de Eland, from whom Lasingcroft derives its name. They were a knightly race, had inter-married with some of the best county families, and lived in a style of great splendour. Their lands were held as a fief under the Earls of Warren, and Sir John, who now represented the family, held the stewardship of the Earl's manors in Yorkshire, including that of Wakefield. He was also the shire-reeve, and, as such, the representative of the King, in the administration of justice and law within the county. Little further is known of him, and he would have scarcely been remembered, but for a deadly feud which arose between him and his above-mentioned neighbours, and a series of atrocious murders arising thereout. Even this might have been forgotten, as at that time deadly fights between families or communities frequently occurred, and excited but little notice, blood-for-blood vengeance being looked upon as a matter of course, and in the same light that duels were a century or two ago. The Livery Companies then frequently met in Cheapside to settle their quarrels with bows and clubs; and the famous fight of Chevy Chase was nothing more than the outcome of a dispute between two border Earls about hunting without permission across the border. So, with other frays of similar character, it might have passed into oblivion, but for a ballad which was written at the time, a modernised version of which appeared *temp.* Henry VIII., and which has come down to the present time— a copy of which was printed in Halifax in 1789, and another published in Whittaker's "Loidis et Elmete." The more modern version was entitled "Revenge upon Revenge: a narrative of the

tragical practices of Sir John Eland, High
Sheriff of Yorkshire, on Sir Robert Beaumont,
in the reign of King Edward III." It gives the
whole of the proceedings, with such circumstantial
detail that, although some authorities have
endeavoured to throw discredit upon the narrative, and expressed their belief that it is a fiction,
it bears internal evidence of its truth. Sir John
was a man of overbearing temper, impatient of
opposition to his behests, and implacable in his
hatred. The ballad opens with a long diatribe on
pride and worldly ambition, and says—

> " With such like faults was found infect
>   One, Sir John Eland, Knight;
> His doings made it much suspect
>   Therein he took delight."

Whilst Sir Robert Beaumont, the main object of
his hatred, is thus mentioned—

> "Sometime there dwelt in Crosland Hall
>   A kind and courteous Knight;
> It was well known that he withal
>   Sir Robert Beaumont hight.
> Some say that Eland Sheriff was
>   By Beaumont disobey'd,
> Which might him make for that trespass
>   With him the worst afraid."

The origin of the feud appears to have been in
this wise—Earl de Warren had seduced Alice de

Lacy, wife of Thomas, Earl of Lancaster, upon which a quarrel arose between the two Earls, and their retainers met and fought, when a nephew of Sir John was slain by one Exley. Exley made over to Sir John a plot of land as compensation for the mischance, which he accepted, but still sought to be avenged by the death of the homicide. Exley fled to the house of his relative, Sir Robert Beaumont, for shelter, and Sir John demanded his surrender, which was refused by Sir Robert, and in this he was countenanced by his friends Quarmby and Lockwood, on the ground that Sir John, having accepted the plot of land, had condoned the offence, which gave great affront to Sir John, who went off muttering threats of vengeance.

Sir John was doubtlessly perfectly right, in his capacity of Sheriff, to demand the delivery up of an offender against the laws of the realm, but he was equally in the wrong in having accepted a bribe to compromise the offence; but his irritation arose from the fact of Sir Robert having set his authority at defiance—an insult which his proud spirit could not brook. He brooded over the matter at home for some days, and at length came to the resolution of erasing

M

the stain upon his dignity by the death of Sir
Robert, which he determined to accomplish with
his own hands.   He considered, further, that
as Quarmby and Lockwood had backed Sir
Robert in his defiance of him as Sheriff, they
would be likely to avenge his death, so, to make
assurance doubly sure, he felt it to be necessary
to deal out the same fate to them.   Accordingly,
a few days after—

> " He raised the country round about,
>   His friends and tenants all,
> And for his purpose picked out
>   Stout, sturdy men, and tall.
> To Quarmby Hall they came by night,
>   And there the lord they slew,
> At that time Hugh of Quarmby hight,
>   Before the country knew.
> To Lockwood then, the selfsame night,
>   They came, and there they slew
> Lockwood of Lockwood, that wiley wight.
>   That stirred the strife anew."

" A gentleman of that wisdom and prudence that
he was not only reckoned, but esteemed, as the
oracle, as well as the darling, of his country, and
whose memory will remain fragrant in future
ages."

Having completed these preliminary murders,
Sir John proceeded with his men to execute his

coup de grace.   Crosland Hall was surrounded by
a deep moat—

> " The hall was watered well about,
>   No wight might enter in,
> Till that the bridge was well made out
>   They durst not enter in."

As the bridge was raised, they lay in ambush till
early in the morning, when it was lowered to
allow a maid-servant to pass forth, upon which
they rushed across and entered the house in a
noisy, boisterous manner. Sir Robert came from
his chamber, half-dressed, to ascertain the cause
of the disturbance, when he was attacked by the
invaders of his premises. He seized a sword and
stood on his defence—

> " And thus it was, most certainly,
>   That slain before he was
> He fought again them manfully,
>   Undressed though he was.
> His lady cried and shrieked withal
>   When as from her they led
> Her dearest knight into the hall,
>   And there cut off his head."

A MS. says that Exley and a brother of Sir
Robert were killed at the same time.

Sir John then ordered wine and victuals to be
laid out for their breakfast, and invited the two
sons of Sir Robert to sit down and join him in

the repast; the younger, through fear, assented, but Adam, the elder, refused, with a scowling brow, to eat with the murderer of his father, upon seeing which, Sir John said, "How heinously that lad doth take his father's death; and looks with a frowning countenance as if he would take revenge; but I will keep such a watchful, circumspect eye over him that he shall never be able to do us any harm." Having thus accomplished his purpose, and finished his meal beside the corpse of his victim lying on the floor, he departed with his band of assassins, nor does it appear that he was ever called to account for the outrage. After the burial of her husband, Lady Beaumont, fearing for the safety of her children, fled with them to the house of her kinsman, Townley, in Lancashire, and took along with her the sons of Quarmby and Lockwood, and a youth named Lacy, of Crumblebottom, where they were instructed together in feats of chivalry, fencing, tilting, shooting with the long bow, riding, and other knightly qualities, as preparations for taking their revenge.

The curtain had fallen upon the first act of the drama; fifteen years had now elapsed, and the second act commences. The four youths had

now grown up nearly to manhood, and
Lockwood, the eldest, suggested that the time
was now come when "we should bravely seek
to revenge the spilling of our fathers' blood, for
if Eland should have that foul act for well done,
it will encourage him in his wickedness, and
further to proceed in destroying the whole
posterity of our renowned ancestors; therefore
do I esteem it our wisdom, and an undertaking
well becoming the successors of such worthy
patriots, utterly to extirpate from the face of
the earth the cursed Cain and his posterity."
The others assented, and took into their counsel
two men—Dawson and Haigh—retainers of
one of the families—who had come from Yorkshire, and who informed them that Sir John
would shortly go to Brighouse, where the
Sheriffdom was to be held, and that they might
easily waylay him and accomplish their purpose.
Accordingly they set off, accompanied by an
armed band of men, and secreted themselves
in Crumblebottom Wood, on the wayside from
Eland to Brighouse.

Sir John, suspecting nothing, went on his way
to Brighouse, and coming upon some armed men
on the roadside whom he knew not, courteously

"vail'd his bonnet," when Adam Beaumont
stepped forward and said—

> "Thy courtesy 'vails thee not, Sir Knight,
>   Thou slew my father dear,
> Sometime Sir Robert Beaumont hight;
>   And slain thou shalt be here."

The others addressed him in like terms.
"Whose fathers' blood," said they all, "we are
now come to revenge upon thee and thine."
They then attacked him, his followers drawing
their weapons and rallying round him in his
defence, and a general fight commenced between
the two companies, several on both sides being
wounded. At length the four young men, who
kept together, succeeded in separating Sir John
from his followers, and inflicting upon him
numerous wounds, left him lying bleeding and
dying upon the turf. Knowing that such a
crime as the murder of the King's Sheriff could
not pass unnoticed, as soon as they felt assured
that they had accomplished their revenge
they hastened back into Lancashire, but
feeling that they would not be safe at
Townley Hall, they went onward into Furness,
then a wild unfrequented corner of the county,
with few inhabitants excepting the monks of the

abbey and a few peasants who were dependent upon it, and hid themselves in the recesses of the woods, among the caves and fells, depending upon their bows for the supply of their daily food. And thus ends the second act of the drama.

In the meanwhile, Sir John's son, a second Sir John, succeeded to Eland, who was married and had a son, then a young boy, who might also have succeeded but for the machinations of the allies in Furness. During the winter they had been laying their plots, and came to the determination of utterly extirpating the male line of the Elands, and arranged to attack Sir John on his way to or from church on Palm Sunday. Accordingly, in the spring, they came secretly to Crumblebottom Hall, where they lay *perdu* to watch events, and, on the eve of Palm Sunday, concealed themselves in Eland Mill. Their proceedings, however, were not so secret but that rumours of impending evil reached the ears of Sir John, and on Sunday morning he told his wife that he should not go out that day, but she rallied him on his fears, and urged that he must go to church on that specially holy day as an example to others, upon which he

reluctantly assented, but took the precaution
of putting on a coat of mail beneath his waist-
coat.

The confederates and their followers saw the
sun rise on the morning of Palm Sunday as they
lay in the mill, and began to prepare for their
meditated deed, when the door was suddenly
opened, and the miller's wife entered for some
corn which her husband had sent her for.   They
immediately seized her, bound her hand and foot,
and told her that if she cried out they would
knock her on the head.   Not returning in due
course, her husband grew wroth at her dalliance.

> "The milner swore she should repent,
>   She tarried there so long;
> A good cudgel in hand he went,
>   To chastise her with wrong."

But the miller, instead of amusing himself by
thrashing his wife, met with the same fate that
she had undergone, and was thrown, securely
bound, on a heap of flour-sacks beside her.

Sir John, his wife, and little son, left Eland
Hall for church, taking a short cut over the
stones of the mill-dam which was nearly empty
in consequence of a drought.   As he was
stepping over Beaumont shot an arrow at him

which glanced off his coat of mail, as did Lockwood with a like effect. The villagers, who were going to church, seeing this, came running up, when Lockwood shot another arrow, which pierced Sir John's brain, whilst another from Quarmby, mortally wounded the boy.

They had now accomplished their vengeance; the male line of the Elands was extinct; but it behoved them to look to their own safety, as the villagers, armed with clubs and hatchets, were assembling in great force. They rushed out of the mill, fought their way along Whittlelane End to Old Earthgate, and hence to Anely Wood, hotly pursued by their foes. Willet, Smith, Remington, and Bunney, yoemanry officers, also summoned their men, who armed themselves with "pitchforks, long staves, knotted clubs, and rusty bills," and joined the hunt. As their foes neared them, they faced round and presented a bold, resolute front, as long as their arrows lasted, when they again took to flight; Lockwood carrying off Quarmby, who had fallen wounded. They gained the shelter of the wood, where they left Quarmby, dead, and each sought to shift for himself. Beaumont took refuge in Crosland Hall, and stood on his defence with the bridge drawn up ; he afterwards escaped to France, fought against the Turks in Hungary, where he won great fame and honour, and eventually became a Knight of Rhodes. Lockwood sought shelter in Camel Hall, but was captured when incautiously visiting a village maiden with whom he had an amour, and was put to death there and then, and so ended the race of the Lockwoods. What became of Lacy is not known. Sir John Eland, the younger, left a daughter and heiress, who married Sir John Savile, of Tankersley, and conveyed the Eland and other estates to that family.

The Plumpton Marriage.

HE Plumpton family, of Plumpton, near Knaresborough, were established there from the period of the Domesday Book, when Edred de Plumpton held two carucates of land of William de Percy, the mesne lord. They had estates afterwards at other places—Idle, near Leeds, held of the Lacies; Steeton, near Tadcaster; Nesfield, near Otley, where they had a manor-house, and elsewhere. They were a family of considerable importance in Yorkshire, and were great benefactors to the Nunnery of Esholt, in Craven. They frequently make a conspicuous appearance in the various historical events of the centuries of their existence. Peter, son of Nigel, suffered confiscation of his lands for confederating with the Barons against King John; but, on submitting and doing fealty to Henry III., they were restored. Sir Robert, founder of a chapel in the church in Knaresborough, was beheaded at York, for participation in Scrope's rebellion against King Henry IV., in 1408. Sir William, who objected to the levying of tolls, at Otley and Ripley, by Archbishop Kemp, lay in wait for the tax-gatherers at Thornton Bridge, with a company of foresters. The officials, apprehending the meaning of the armed men by the bridge, turned aside to pass over the river by Brafferton Ford, but were followed by Sir William and his men, shouting, "Slay the Archbishop's carles, and would to God we had the Archbishop himself here." In the fray which ensued, several of the Archbishop's men were slain and wounded, and others taken prisoners. Robert, the last male representative of the family, died unmarried and intestate at Paris, in 1749, when the estates passed to his aunt, Anne, who, in 1760, sold them to Daniel Lascelles, for £28,000.

A volume entitled "The Plumpton Correspondence," consisting of family letters, chiefly of a domestic character, written in the reigns of Edward IV., Richard III., Henry VII., and Henry VIII., was published in 1869 by the Camden Society; edited by Thomas Stapleton, from Sir Edward Plumpton's "Book of Letters."

In the reign of Henry II., Gilbert de Plumpton, a youthful scion of the family, was living at Plumpton. As the Plumptons were then comparatively small land-owners, and as they had high aspirations, aiming at the knightly or baronial degree, it behoved them to improve their landed estates by prudent marriages with heiresses, and thus qualify themselves for a higher position in the county. Young Gilbert, then approaching manhood, therefore cast his eyes about him with that purpose. His range of vision was rather restricted, as people in those days, owing to the badness of the roads and other causes, rarely travelled far away from home, and were almost compelled to select their wives and husbands from amongst their neighbours, seldom going beyond the bounds of their native counties to enter into matrimonial alliances. Besides this, eligible heiresses were but few in number, and being under the guardianship of the King, or of some one appointed by him, whose consent was necessary for marriage, it being a serious offence to marry an heiress without such pre-consent, it became a difficult matter, even when an heiress was found and her affections secured, to consummate their reciprocal

love by a conjugal union; especially as Kings
were then wont to use their power over their
fair wards in a very arbitrary and tyrannical
fashion, by bestowing their hands and inheritances
on their favourites, or in reward for some service,
without the least consideration for the pleasure or
will of the person most concerned—the lady
herself.

About this time Roger de Guilevast, or, as he
is sometimes called, Richard Wardwast, a wealthy
land-owner, in the neighbourhood of Plumpton,
died, and left his only daughter, Eleanor, heiress
to his extensive possessions. This young lady,
Gilbert had encountered when out with his hounds
one day, some twelve months previously. He had
been searching for game in the woodlands of the
picturesque scenery which surrounds Plumpton,
and had come to the lake, when he was startled
by the sight of an exquisitely beautiful young
girl wandering along the shore, and seemingly
enjoying the beautiful prospect of land, water,
and foliaged trees. He accosted her, and she
readily entered into conversation with him, when
he was as much struck by her wit and sensible
remarks as he had previously been by her beauty.
She informed him who she was, and who her

father, and he imparted to her the same
information respecting himself, and they discovered
that, although they had never chanced to meet
previously, they were well acquainted with each
other's families. Gilbert therefore knew that if
her father died without other issue his estates
would descend to her as his heiress. Here
he thought was the chance he had been hoping
for; but as he was of a cautious, calculating
disposition, he considered that her father, not yet
aged, might still have a son, to whom the lands
would pass, and leave her with nothing more
than a slender marriage portion; and although
he saw that she was beautiful and accomplished,
and was just the wife whom he would choose
if personal charms were the chief consideration,
he could not, in justice to his family and his own
aspirations, marry a dowerless maiden, and he
resolved not to commit himself too far until he
saw more as to the chance of her succession to
the estates. Still he determined not to lose
sight of her altogether, and that it would be well
in the meantime to inspire her heart with the
sentiment of love towards him, if it were possible
to do so.

"Do you often walk in this direction?" he asked.

"Oh yes," she replied, "in the beautiful summer sunshine, when the trees are clad in their bright vestments of green, and the flowers are opening their petals and giving forth perfume from every bank; when the birds are singing joyfully overhead, and the hum of the bees and other insects add a pleasing undertone to their louder carolling—I love to wander alone with Nature for my companion. And you! Do you care to commune with Nature? or only feel a pleasure in going forth in the forest lands and pastures, to destroy the innocent and beautiful creatures who enjoy their existence as much as you do yourself?" And so saying, she pointed interrogatively at his dogs, which were barking and sniffing about among the bushes.

"Oh!" answered he, "believe not that my sole delight is in the chase. Nature has sent certain animals into the world to supply us with food, and it is right to deprive them of life before placing them on the table; nor do I think it wrong to destroy noxious animals, such as wolves and foxes, and it is only on such that I wage war; nothing do I kill out of wanton sport. I experience pleasure in the sight of the rising and the setting sun, I can look with delight on the glories of a landscape, such as that which is spread around us, and witness with a thrill of sublime awe the warring of the elements in a tempest."

Thus they conversed for some time, mutually interested in each other's conversation, and before parting arranged to meet at set times near the huge rock which rises out of the water and stretches for a length of fifty feet, and which still attracts thousands of tourists to wonder at and admire it.

Many times did they meet there, and their love ripened at each interview, Gilbert almost forgetting the demands of his family for heiresses, and almost resolving to seek her hand, even in case of a brother coming to claim the inheritance ; but some six months afterwards, Eleanor's father "went the way of all flesh," and she became really an heiress, when Gilbert commenced making love to her in real earnest, his own private inclinations coinciding now with what was due to his consideration of the interests of his family.

At this time Ranulph de Glanville was resident in Yorkshire, as Lord of Coverdale, having acquired the estates there by his marriage with

N

Bertha, daughter of Theobald de Valvins, Lord of Parham. He was the greatest legal luminary of his age, and eminent, besides, as a statesman and warrior; was Judge-itinerant in Yorkshire and thirteen other counties, and in 1186 was promoted to the dignity of Chief-Justice of England; he was also Sheriff of Yorkshire and some other counties, and was employed extensively in State affairs. When King Henry II. was in France, King William of Scotland invaded Northumberland, in 1174, and Glanville, as Sheriff of Yorkshire, raised an army of Yorkshiremen, marched against him, defeated him in a battle, and took him prisoner, lodging him in Richmond Castle. News of the victory reached the King after his memorable penance at the tomb of Thomas a Becket, and, instead of attributing it to the skill of Glanville and the bravery of his followers, ascribed it to St. Thomas, as a reward for his penitential humiliation at his shrine. In his latter days he founded an abbey and a priory in his native county of Suffolk; in 1189 he accompanied King Richard in his crusade to Palestine, and is said to have been slain at the siege of Acre.

As Sheriff of the county of York, he was the

representative of the King, and, of course, in the matter of the guardianship of heiresses and the disposal of their hands and inheritances. When intelligence reached him of the death of Roger de Guilevast without issue male, it occurred to him that it would be a good opportunity for rewarding one, Reiner, a favourite dependant of his, whom he wished to advance in life. Reiner is mentioned in the Plump. Cartul., 1002, as Sheriff of Yorkshire, but as Glanville himself was then Sheriff, he would probably be Deputy-Sheriff. He therefore proposed to bestow the heiress and her estates upon Reiner, and gave instructions to that effect.

The lovers, for plighted lovers they had become when Eleanor received an intimation that she was to give her hand to Reiner, resolved upon a bold step, no less than that of defying the King and his Sheriff by a clandestine marriage. Gilbert was on terms of great intimacy with the Spofforths of Spofforth, a township adjoining that of Plumpton, an ancient Saxon family, one of whom, Thomas, early in the fifteenth century, became Abbot of St. Mary's, York, and, in 1422, was elected Bishop of Rochester, but, before installation, was constituted

Bishop of Hereford by Papal provision. One of the family was a priest and the close friend of Gilbert, and he undertook to risk the performance of the ceremony, which was carried out in private, and Gilbert took his bride home, and for a week or more enjoyed the usual connubial felicity of the honeymoon period.

A loud knocking at the gates of the Plumpton Manor House one morning startled the inmates and aroused the fears of the newly married couple, who were apprehensive of the vengeance of the Sheriff. At first they thought of flight; but where to go? Nowhere in the realm would they be safe against the power of the King, so they were compelled perforce to abide the issue. When the gates were opened, a body of men in the livery of the Sheriff presented themselves, the leader of whom said, " In the name of the King, and by the authority of his Sheriff, Ranulph de Glanville, I demand to be delivered up to me the bodies of Gilbert de Plumpton and of Eleanor de Guilevast, a ward of the Crown, who has been treacherously carried off from her home by the said Gilbert, in violation of the laws of the realm, and in traitorous contempt of the King's authority."

At this juncture Gilbert presented himself with his wife leaning on his arm, and demanded what they meant by such intrusion and insolent language, adding that he was no traitor and no contemner of the laws of the kingdom, but one of the King's most faithful subjects.

"We come not," was the reply, "to bandy words with you, or decide the question at issue; our instructions are to convey you to York, where the Sheriff will determine what further shall be done in the matter, and who will listen to any objections you may be pleased to urge in respect of your apprehension as a violator of the law."

Seeing that there was no use in resisting, Gilbert said, "Then I will accompany you to York," and gave directions for his horse to be saddled. "But," he continued, "I trust it is not necessary to submit this lady, my wife, to the indignity; I suppose she may remain here until I have vindicated my innocence, and can return to her."

"That cannot be," replied the leader, "my instructions are to bring you and the lady, and loth as I am to appear discourteous to a lady, I must insist on her accompanying us."

"I am ready to go," said Eleanor; "rather would I go to face any perils, in your company, than 'be left behind with all the anxieties and uncertainties as to what is befalling you."

Another horse was then brought from the stables for her accommodation, and the party rode together to York. They were placed in the custody of the Sheriff's officers, but not in prison, and a few days after were brought before the Sheriff. He interrogated Gilbert with great severity, who acknowledged the marriage, and the lady with more courtesy, who replied with modesty, pleading that she was not aware that marrying the man to whom she had given her heart could be a matter of offence to the King, adding that, so far as she knew, even a milkmaid or a peasant girl was at liberty to marry whom she chose. The Sheriff explained that she was very different from a peasant girl, who was a mere serf, and that it mattered not whom she married, but that she was an inheritor of a portion of the land of England, the whole of which belonged to the King, and that such being the case, it was necessary for the welfare of the realm that he should have in his hand the disposal of such heiresses in marriage, so that their estates should not fall into the hands of unworthy persons. " I can understand," he continued, " that you, a simple maiden, should be ignorant of this essential feature of the constitution of the realm, and being so, are entitled rather to compassion than blame for having been inveigled into this unlawful marriage, which, in the eye of the law, is no marriage at all, but concubinage. As for you, sir," addressing himself to Gilbert, " you are supposed to be cognisant of the laws of the land, and have been guilty of a gross crime and misdemeanour, which may lead to serious consequences. It will be necessary for me to lay the matter before the King's grace, and bring you before his tribunal of justice, so that he may deal with you as he deems fitting, and rest assured, it will go well with you if you escape with your life. As for your wife, as you call her, it is probable you will never more see her ; but she will be well cared for, if that be any consolation to you, and shall be provided with a suitable and worthy husband." On hearing this announcement, Eleanor uttered a piercing shriek, and fell fainting to the floor. She was carried away into an adjoining apartment, whilst her husband, betraying signs of deep agitation, attempted to speak, but was prevented doing so by direction of the Judge.

What followed may be told in the words of the Plumpton MS. :—In the year 1184, while the King (Henry II.) was sojourning at Worcester with his army, with intent to make war with Rhys-ap-Griffin, a certain youth was brought there in fetters, sprung of noble lineage, and whose name was Gilbert de Plumpton, whom Ranulph de Glanville, the King's justiciary, had in odium, and sought to put to death, laying to his charge that he had ravished a certain maiden in the King's gift, the daughter of Roger de Guilevast, and kept her to him as his wife, and that, in the night-time, he broke through six doors in the abode of the girl's father, and took a hunting-horn and a head-stall, etc., along with the said maiden. He added, moreover, that all these things he carried off by theft and robbery, and upon the issue he offered to abide the law. But Ranulph de Glanville, wishing to make away with him, because he designed to give the same maiden (whom the said Gilbert had already known after their espousals) to Reiner, Sheriff of Yorkshire,

with her father's inheritance, further exhorted
those who were to try Gilbert to adjudge him to
death ; and so it was done, for they sentenced
him to be hanged, and whilst he was being led to
the gibbet, intelligence was brought of the
proceedings in his case to Baldwin, Bishop of the
same city of Worcester. The which Bishop,
though in great grief for the condemnation of the
youth, was, however, exhorted by his attendants
to rescue him from death. They said that he
could legally do this, because it was a Sunday
the same day, and upon it the Feast of Blessed
Mary Magdalen. The Bishop (who was a meek
and good man) acquiesced in their arguments,
and having mounted on horseback, quickly rode
after the executioners, who were leading the
youth to the gibbet, and had now arrived at the
place. Already was the youth, with his hands
bound behind his back, and with a green band
covering his eyes, and an iron chain round his
neck—the executioners being on the point of
hoisting the youth up as the Bishop arrived with
a multitude of people.

Having alighted from his horse, and running
up, he stationed himself by the side of the
prisoner, thus exclaiming and saying, "I forbid

you, on the part of God and the blessed Mary Magdalen, and under sentence of excommunication, to hang this man on this day; because to-day is the day of our Lord and the feast of the blessed Mary Magdalen. Wherefore it is not lawful for you to contaminate the day."

The executioners replied, "Who are you, and what madness prompts you that you have the audacity to impede the execution of the King's justice?" But the Bishop, with no less firmness of heart than of speech, rejoins, "Not madness, but the clemency of heavenly pity, urges me; nor do I desire to impede the King's justice, but to warn against an unwary act, lest by the contamination of a solemn day, you and the King incur the wrath of the Eternal God."

After some altercation, divine authority at length prevailed; and at the entreaty of the Bishop, he who was bound was unloosed; nevertheless he was delivered over to the keeper of the King's castle in safe custody, and in the morning to be led again to execution. But the Lord Almighty, who never deserts those who hope in Him, granted longer span of life to the said Gilbert. For when all these matters were reported to King Henry, he sent his messengers in the greatest haste to the castle with orders that the youth should not be hanged.

This story is deemed apochryphal by some authorities as being utterly inconsistent with the mild, beneficent, and just character of the Justiciary. Foss, who refers to it as a dereliction from the path of judicial integrity, says— " Presuming the story to be true, the Chief Justiciary's merit must have been great indeed to induce the King to pardon so monstrous a perversion of justice," adding, " some doubt, however, cannot but be attached to the relation, not merely from its extravagant ferocity and the impunity of its perpetrators, but from the assertion of the work which bears Glanville's name, who says—" None of the Judges have so hardened a front, or so rash a presumption, as to dare to deviate, however slightly, from the path of justice, or utter a sentence in any measure contrary to the truth." It is scarcely possible to suppose that a King so just as Henry II. would have overlooked the guilt of the Judge, or have visited the innocence of the accused with imprisonment.

On the other side, Roger de Hoveden relates the story with some circumstantiality, under the date of 1184, who was not only a contemporary, but was a native of Howden, not many miles distant from Plumpton. He adds further, that " The Knight (Gilbert) being rescued from death, was kept in prison by Ranulph de Glanville until the King's death (1189)." In the Annals of the Exchequer also, we find given the expenses of conveying Gilbert de Plumpton from York to Worcester, on this occasion.

What became of Gilbert and Eleanor afterwards is not recorded, or mentioned in the tradition, but we may hope that after his release on the accession of Richard I., they were re-united, and that their oppressor, having died the following year, they were enabled to pass the remainder of their lives in tranquility and happiness.

The Topcliffe Insurrection.

"I wayle, I wepe, I sobbe, I sighe full sore,
The dedely fate, the dolefulle destenny
Of him that is gone, alas ! without restore,
Of the blode royall descendinge nobelly ;
Whos lordshepe doutles was slayne lamentably,
Thorow tresen ageyn hym compassyd and wrought,
Trew to his Prince, in worde, in dede, and thought."

—SKELTON.

THE prevailing blemish in the character of King Henry VII. was avarice, which led him, through his rapacious ministers, Empson and Dudley, to oppress the people with extortionate taxation. To save his exchequer he avoided foreign wars, and once only did he cross the sea with that object, in the cause of Anne of Bretagne, whose fief was claimed by the French King ; but on arriving at Boulogne, King Charles, appealing to his master-passion, bought him off by means of a large bribe. For the purpose of this war, Parliament, in February, 1489, granted a tax of one-tenth of a penny, for a subsidy of £75,000. This oppressive

tax was very unpopular, and especially so in
Yorkshire and the north, the people about Thirsk,
particularly, being loud in their murmurs. They
were goaded on by the rough and excited
harangues of one John à Chambre, whom Lord
Bacon describes as "a base fellow called John
Chambre, a very brute feu, who bore most sway
among the vulgar." He had for his fellow leader
Sir John Egremont, who, although not quite so
boisterous and unpolished as Chambre, was
equally resolute and vigorous in his opposition to
fiscal extortion; and these two leaders gathered
around them a body of rustics and mechanics,
who armed themselves with such weapons as
they could procure, such as scythes, bill-hooks,
and bludgeons. Vowing they would not lay down
their arms until the tax was repealed, they went
from village to village, and town to town,
inveighing against the King's evil counsellors,
explaining their designs, and enlisting recruits to
their banner.

An account of these turbulent proceedings
reached the ears of the King, who sent an order
down to the Earl of Northumberland, the Lord-
Lieutenant of Yorkshire, to explain the necessity
of the tax, to uphold the honour and dignity of

the nation. The Earl wrote back to the King a letter of remonstrance, showing that the tax was intolerably oppressive, a burden that they were scarcely able to bear, and praying him to re-consider it, and make some abatement in the demand. To this he received a reply that not a single penny should be abated, and he was enjoined to see that it was exacted to the utter-most farthing.

Henry Percy, fourth Earl of Northumberland, was one of the most potent nobles of the north, and had castles at Topcliffe, on the Swale, near Thirsk; at Leckonfield, near Beverley; and at Wressil, near Howden—all maintained with a splendour almost regal, with barons, knights, and esquires as members of his household and retinue. The Castle of Topcliffe, the earliest and chief seat of the Percies, stood with its massive keep, battlemented towers, gateway, walls, and dungeon, upon an elevated mound called Maiden Bower, on the river Swale, near the confluence of the Cod-beck. From its nearness to Thirsk, the focus of the insurrection, the Earl came thither from Leckonfield to execute the command of the King, and he called a folk-môte at Thirsk for that purpose. With his vassals and tenants

he was popular, being a kind and considerate
master and landlord, and by the people of Yorkshire he was held in high esteem, so that he was
under no apprehension, although the people were
in arms; and he took no measures for his safety
in case of tumult, feeling assured that there was
no danger, and that he would be able, by his
explanations and expostulations, to appease the
angry feelings of the multitude.

On the morning of the day appointed for the
meeting, there was a great assemblage of people
in Thirsk, and excited crowds coming along all
the roads leading thither from Ripon, Boroughbridge, Easingwold, and the neighbouring
villages. The people were armed chiefly with
bludgeons, and displayed two banners, one in-
scribed "No taxes; down with Empson and
Dudley," the other, "Oh for the days of good
King Dickon." Richard III., when residing at
Middleham, as Duke of Gloucester, was exceed
ingly popular with the poor, mingling with them
in their amusements, and consorting with them
as familiarly as if they were his equals, probably
with a politic eye to the future. When he was
carrying out his scheme of usurpation, he sent
for a contingent of men-at-arms from his

Middleham estates, who assembled for review in Finsbury Fields, when one of his Yorkshire tenants stepped out of the ranks, and, clapping him on the shoulder, said, "Ah's main blythe thoo's goin' to be King, Dickon."

Egremont and Chambre were in the midst on horseback, riding hither and thither, exhorting the people with inflammatory speeches to be firm in their determination not to pay the tax, telling them that all England was with them, and not to listen to the Earl, who was one of the King's advisers in levying the tax; further, that if need be they would lead them to London and compel the King to remit the tax, or drag him from his throne.

At this time the Earl rode into the town, surrounded by a body of retainers, all men of rank, habited in brilliant costume, the livery of the Percies. He was assailed with mingled cheers from his tenants, and hisses and shouts of opprobrium from the insurgent mob. He attempted to address them, but the uproar became greater; again he made the attempt, when there arose a deafening discord of sounds from drums, kettles, and pans, accompanied by the yelling and howling of the mob, when,

finding he could not gain their ear, he and his
followers turned their horses' heads and trotted
back to Topcliffe. As they passed away, the
leaders shouted, " Bravely done, my merry men ;
this is our first victory; let us on to Topcliffe,
and beard him in his castle, and then for London,
to face the tyrant King in the Tower." The
Earl and his followers gained the castle, and
were seated in consultation on what were best to
be done in the emergency, when loud shouts
assailed their ears from outside, and, looking forth,
they perceived that they had been followed by
the mob, infuriated by the harangues of their
leaders. Although implored not to do so, but to
shut the gates and stand a siege, the Earl went
out and faced the insurgents.

" What want you, good people ? " he inquired.

"A remission of the tax," replied Egremont.

" I have no power or authority to do so," said
the Earl.

" Who but you advised the King that not a
penny should be abated ?" shouted Chambre,
and the mob yelled, and cried, " Down with him ;
he wants to rob our children of their bread."

The Earl was a proud man, and scorned to
give a denial to the insinuation, which served

to inflame the passions of the rioters to a still higher degree.

"He's silent, and that proves his guilt," shouted Chambre. "Down with him; such bloodsuckers should not be allowed to exist."

And then there was a brandishing of clubs and a rush forward of the mob, and in a few moments the Earl was stricken down, and beaten savagely as he lay. The mob then entered the castle tumultuously, and killed several of his domestics; but the barons and knights, fled to seek safety, or, as Skelton has it—

> "Trustinge in noblemen, that wer wyth hym there;
> Bot all they fled from hym from falshode or fere,
> He was envyronde aboute on every syde,
> Withe his enemys that were stark mad and wode;
> Yet whils he stode he gave them woundes wyde,
> Alas! for southe! what thoughe his mynde were goode,
> His courage manly; yet there he shed his bloode.
> All left alone, alas! he fowt in vayne,
> For cruelly among them ther he was slayne."

Hence the insurgents went triumphantly, calling upon the people to unite with them in putting down kingly tyranny and financial oppression, but eventually they were met by the Earl of Surrey, who was sent against them, at Ackworth, near Pontefract, and dispersed. Chambre and others of the leaders were captured and hanged

at York; but Egremont, thanks to the fleetness
of his horse, escaped to Flanders, and was
protected by the Yorkist Margaret, Duchess of
Burgundy. What was his ultimate fate is not
known.

The Earl was honoured with a most magnificent funeral in the Minster or Collegiate Church
of St. John, Beverley, in a chapel built expressly
for the reception of his remains, and beneath a
tomb with rich Gothic canopy, adorned with
sculptured figures, and emblazoned with the
multitude of quarterings of the family. The
body, after having been embalmed, was conveyed
to his Castle of Wressil, and hence to Leckonfield,
whence it was taken to Beverley, accompanied
by a long and splendid procession, all robed
and accoutred at the expense of the family.
There were twelve lords with "gownes at 10s.
the yerd;" twenty-four lords and knights "with
gownes and hods;" sixty squires and gentlemen
"with gownes and typets;" two hundred yeomen
"in gownes;" "one hundred gromes and gentlemen's servants in gownes." There were also
the bearers of the great standard, twelve bearers
of sarcenet banners "betyn with my Lord's
armys," sixty bearers of "Scutchions of Buckram

betyn with my Lord's armys," and two officers of arms from the Herald's Office, London, to superintend the armorial arrangements, who were paid £20 for "their helpe and payne." Besides these there were five hundred priests, one thousand clerks, and representatives from the neighbouring monasteries, all habited in mourning, and bearing crucifixes, other church ornaments, and vessels and emblems of mortality. Mingling with these were four hundred torch-bearers, and bringing up the rear, 13,340 poor persons, who received, according to the will, a funeral dole of twopence each. Altogether the cost amounted to £1,037 6s. 8d., equal to, at least, £10,000 of the present value of money.

The body was met at the great west door of the Minster by the Provost, Vicars, Canons, choristers, and other officials of the Minster, who conducted the procession. A mournful anthem was chanted up the nave into the chancel, where a long and splendid service of masses and choral singing was performed, and the body lowered into its resting-place, amid the sobs and lamentations of those who had known and loved the Earl for his virtues. Of his tomb, with its " multiplicity of noble carved work and canopied arches," as described by Leland, there remain only the altar table, with its sides covered with armorial bearings, but without the figures which ranged round it in niches, and on the wall above the word "Esperance," the motto of the family, and "1494," the date of the funeral.

The Burning of Cottingham Castle.

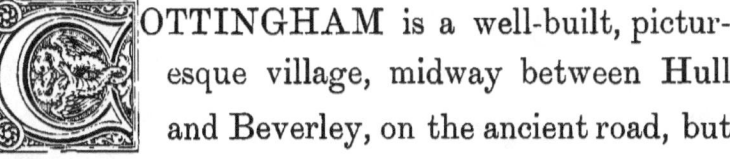OTTINGHAM is a well-built, pictur-esque village, midway between Hull and Beverley, on the ancient road, but a quarter of a mile distant from the modern highway. It is a place of great antiquity, dating from the ancient British period, and deriving its name from Ket, a Celtic female deity, with the Saxon suffixes of ing and ham. In the days of Edward the Confessor, it belonged to one Gamel, who is supposed to have held a Thursday market there; and at the time of the Domesday Book, the manor, four miles in length, with five fisheries of 8,000 eels, was held by Hugh, son of Baldrick.

It was granted by William the Conqueror to Robert de Stuteville, surnamed Front de Bœuf, from whom it descended to Robert de Stuteville, or d'Estoteville, who was Sheriff of Yorkshire, twenty-first Henry II., and from him to William de Stuteville, *temp.* John, who, for some offence, was excommunicated by the Archbishop of York. He appealed to the King, who came to Cottingham to investigate the matter, and in the sequel compelled the prelate to give him absolution. Moreover, he granted to de Stuteville a charter empowering him to castellate his manor-house, and hold a weekly market and annual fair.

Nicholas de Stuteville died seventeenth Henry III., leaving two daughters, Joan and Margaret, as his co-heiresses, the former of whom married Hugh de Wake, descended from Leofric, viceroy Earl of Mercia, and his wife the famous Godiva, and from Hereward le Wac (the Wake), Lord of Brunne, the last, and one of the most formidable, opponents of the Norman Duke William, in his conquest of England. John, his grandson, was summoned as a baron twenty-third Edward I., whose daughter, Margaret, married Edmund of Woodstock, Earl of Kent, third son of King Edward I., and had issue, Joan, "the fair maid of Kent," who inherited the Barony of Wake, which she transmitted to her issue by her first husband, Thomas de Holand, and which fell in abeyance in 1497, as it still continues. She married, secondly, Edward, the

Black Prince, and by him was mother of King Richard II.

King Edward I. was celebrating Christmas with the Wakes at Cottingham, when, being out hunting, he came to Wyke-super-Hull, and, struck with its capabilities as a port, granted the charter which laid the foundation of its future greatness, and changed its name to Kingstown-upon-Hull; and at the same time gave his host a charter of free warren over his manor, and authority to erect a gallows for the execution of criminals. Thomas, his son, in the following reign, obtained a charter of confirmation, with the privilege of holding a weekly market and two annual fairs, and authority to convert his residence into a castle of defence, and to garrison it with armed men. This Thomas founded, adjacent to the castle, a monastery of Austin Friars, on a site with a defective title, in consequence of which it was removed to Haltem-price, on another part of the estate.

The feudal barony was held *in capite* by the service of one barony, and consisted of 4,000 acres, with £200 yearly rental from free tenants.

It was a beautiful August day in the year 1540. The reapers were in the fields about

Cottingham, sickle in hand, cutting down the golden corn, and lumbering wains with solid wooden wheels, and drawn by oxen, were carrying away the sheaves to garner in the home-steads; the fruit of a thousand trees in the orchards surrounding the village hung, rich and luscious, pendant from the boughs, and ripening to perfection under the bright sunshine. The village consisted of a scattering of cross-timbered houses with wattled and mud-walled frames, latticed windows, and thatched roofs. From the midst thereof rose in proud and lofty dignity the majestic walls, turrets, and bastions of the Stutevilles, the Wakes, and now of the Holands, surrounded by a moat, which was crossed by a drawbridge, and the entrance defended by a barbican and a portcullis. Upon its battlements might be seen three or four men-at-arms, lounging lazily about, and amusing themselves by watching the passage of vessels and boats up and down the Humber. The pleasant clack of the baronial mill, and the occasional uplifted voices of the denizens of the farm-yards and pastures, alone broke the silence of the slumberous summer afternoon. In a hamlet within ken of the out-lookers on the parapets of the castle might be

seen the now deserted house of the Augustinian
Friars, at Haltemprice; for here no longer the
Canons dropped their beads, muttered their
prayers, or chanted their anthems; the ruthless
hand of Henry had driven them forth upon the
wide world to become supplicants for charity,
alongside those who had erstwhile found succour
at their gate. The priory and site had in the
present year been granted to Thomas Culpepper,
but he had not yet taken possession, and it lay
desolate and silent, as did, at the same time,
many another noble abbey and priory, scattered
over the face of England. .

Lord Wake, as he was called by courtesy,
although he was only a tenure Baron, had been
out in the direction of the now thriving town of
Kingston-upon-Hull, and about the middle of the
afternoon he came riding over the drawbridge,
and passed through the arched gateway into the
courtyard of his castle. Upon his fist he carried
a favourite hawk, and he was accompanied by his
falconer, and three or four liveried retainers. He
leaped agilely from his horse, which was taken
charge of by a groom, and, handing his hawk to
the falconer, he passed through a portal to the
domestic apartments, where he was met by his

wife, a singularly beautiful woman, not much past
the bloom of girlhood, and as modest, chaste, and
pious as she was charming in feature, person, and
demeanour. " What sport have you had this
morning, husband mine ? " inquired she, after an
affectionate embrace. " Excellent, " he replied;
" my falcon has done wonders, he brought down a
heron, who, from his size, must have been the
patriarch of the shaw ; but, dearest life ! sport of
that kind, brave as it may be, is as naught to the
happiness I experience in thy dear society."
Other expressions of endearment of a similar
kind passed as they sat down to dinner, composed chiefly of venison and boar's flesh. Lord
Wake was a great hunter in the surrounding
woods of his domain, and as he sat at dinner he
was surrounded by half a dozen petted boar and
stag hounds, who gambolled at will about the
apartment, or sat on their haunches, looking up
at their master in anxious expectation of stray
bones, which were thrown to them with no
niggard hand.

The meal passed over almost in silence, which
was only broken occasionally by remarks and discussion on domestic topics ; but when it was
finished, and Lady Wake had taken up her

embroidery-frame, her husband told her that his sport had brought him to the gates of Kingstown, where he learnt that the King was in the town, who had arrived there unexpectedly. He was on his progress to York to meet his nephew, James V. of Scotland, and had come by a circuitous route " for fear of the enraged people," who, exasperated at the dissolution of the religious houses, and the King's assumption of supremacy over the Church, had two or three years previously raised a formidable insurrection, which they denominated the " Pilgrimage of Grace." The Mayor (Henry Thurcross), Lord Wake said, had sent the Sheriff to meet his Highness at the " boarded bridge" of Newland, on the confines . of the county of Hull; had himself, with the aldermen, received him with great obeisance and due formalities at Beverley-gate, and had conducted him to the Manor Hall, the usual residence of Royalty when in the town, where he now was enjoying the splendid hospitality of the Corporation.

" The caitiff," exclaimed Lady Wake, " what does he want down here ? His presence betokens no good, and woe betide those with whom he sojourns."

" Bluff King Hal," as he was frequently termed, was no favourite with the better class of ladies; and especially with such as were of a devout turn of mind, and were regular and punctual in the performance of their religious duties, as enjoined by their father-confessors. His propensity for chopping off the heads of his wives, or of divorcing them when a new beauty enthralled his amorous susceptibilities, caused him to be held in detestation by all right-minded women; and his sacrilegious deposition of the Holy Father's authority in England, combined with his so-called brutal dispersion of the religious fraternities and sisterhoods of the realm, and unwarrantable plunder of the holy places of the land, caused him to be looked upon by the devout as an incarnation of Satan. Such were the views of Lady Wake, who felt keenly the loss of Haltemprice, which had been to her a sanctuary of heaven, and to which she had been a most generous benefactor.

Whilst Lord and Lady Wake were conversing on this subject, the sound of a trumpet was heard outside, followed by the opening of the great gate at the summons, " In the King's name," and the clatter of a horse's hoofs over the drawbridge and into the courtyard. Lord Wake hastened out and found an herald seated on horseback, who, when he announced himself as the lord of the castle, gave three blasts of his trumpet, and then delivered his message :—" His Highness the King Henry, the eighth of the name, by the grace of God, defender of the faith, and supreme head of the Church of England, to the Lord of the Barony of Cottingham, usually styled Lord Wake, greeting—It is His Highness's pleasure that on the morrow he will come, God willing, to Baynard Castle, and partake of the hospitality of the noble Baron and Lady Wake. God save the King." In the the course of conversation with the magnates of Hull, at the Manor Hall, he had made inquiry respecting persons of note residing in the neighbourhood, and Lord Wake was mentioned as keeping up a magnificent establishment within three or four miles of the gates of Hull, and as being blessed with a wife of surpassing beauty. The King's licentious propensities were at once aroused at hearing this. " Fore God," quoth he, " I will betake me thither, and with mine own eyes see whether this Yorkshire beauty is the paragon you represent her to be ; " and he summoned his herald into his presence and despatched him with the above message to Cottingham.

Lord Wake was thrown into consternation at receiving the King's greeting and message, and, before giving an answer, went indoors to consult his wife.

"Holy Mary!" said she, "what a disaster! We must avoid it in some way or other. Never will I meet the woman-slayer and desecrator of God's temples within these walls."

"True," he replied, "we must find some means of averting it if possible, but meanwhile it will be necessary to send a civil and loyal reply," and returning to the courtyard, he bade the herald inform the King that he felt highly flattered at His Highness's condescension in proposing a visit to his humble house, and that on the following day preparations should be made for greeting him in the best way his humble means afforded. When the herald had departed, Lord Wake pondered deeply on the dilemma in which he found himself placed by the King's proffered visit. He felt that it was impossible, except by taking some desperate step, to evade it, but something must be done, as he felt assured that the honour of himself and that of his wife were at stake, well knowing, as he did, the unbridled passion of the King, and that if it were thwarted the most perilous consequences might ensue. The confiscation of his estates might be looked for in such case; but better, thought he, lose my land, than my wife her honour. This train of thought led him to think of his castle, where he had lived so happily with the beloved of his heart, when suddenly the idea struck him—What if I burn down my castle! The King could not come for entertainment amidst its ruined walls and smoking embers, and though I should sacrifice my home, I should preserve what is far dearer to me—my wife, pure and undefiled as when I led her to the altar. The more he thought of the project, the more fully he became assured of its practicability as an effectual bar of defence against the King's intentions. He submitted the idea to Lady Wake, who, without the slightest hesitation, concurred in the proposal.

The seneschal of the castle was then called in—a faithful old retainer, who had been in the family for two or three generations of lords, and who might be intrusted with the keeping of

P

any secret of his master. He was informed of the nature of the peril hanging over the family, and of the method projected by Lord Wake to avert the evil. He had been born and bred up in the castle; knew every nook and corner of it; loved it with a devoted affection, almost as if it had been a thinking, sentient being; and could not without an excess of grief see it destroyed; yet he recognised at once the necessity of the case, and not being able to devise an alternative, so as to save the old towers and walls, undertook, as proposed by his master, to fire the castle that night.

Lord and Lady Wake then proceeded to pack up all the more portable articles of value, jewels, money, family papers, and heirlooms, which were conveyed secretly to the unoccupied Priory of Haltemprice, and thither they went themselves, issuing from a postern, and crossing the moat by means of a raft stationed there for the purpose. When the retainers, men-at-arms, and domestics, all save the sentinals on duty, had retired to rest, the seneschal, heaped together a quantity of combustible materials in proximity to a mass of old and dry woodwork panelling on the walls, which he set fire to. The flames soon caught hold of the woodwork, which, blazing up, got a complete hold of the building. He then rang the alarm-bell and roused up the sleepers, telling them that he had been awakened by the smell of burning. Of course all was done that could be done, under his direction, for the subjugation of the fire, but the appliances were so utterly inefficient, consisting merely of a line of men passing a chain of buckets from hand to hand after being filled from the moat, that the fire soon overcame all their efforts to extinguish it, and the roof soon after falling in, it blazed up into the midnight sky, illuminating the country for miles round. The flames were distinctly visible from Hull and Beverley, and numbers of persons from both towns hurried to the scene of disaster, but could afford no assistance, the fire having by that time gained such an ascendency that they could but stand and gaze, awe-stricken, on the scene of devastation. Intelligence was conveyed to the King the following morning of the " accidental" fire at Baynard Castle, and to show his sympathy he offered to contribute £2,000 towards its restoration, which was respectfully declined by Lord Wake, and the King, after sundry measures for the improvement of the port of Kingstown, crossed the Humber and returned to London.

The tradition adds, further, that this Lord Wake, dying without issue male, the manor was divided between his three daughters, who were respectively married to the Duke of Richmond, the Earl of Westmoreland, and Baron Powis, and that those portions thus acquired the names they still bear of Cottingham Richmond, Cottingham Westmoreland, and Cottingham Powis.

Tradition, however, is prone to error, and in this narrative there are several discrepancies and anachronisms. There was then no Baron Wake, the barony having fallen into abeyance more than a century previously; but the holder of the manor, being a feudal Baron, might bear the title by courtesy. Secondly, Leland saw the ruins of the burnt castle in 1538, two or three years before the visit of King Henry to Hull, and he mentions the division of the manor into four parts as having taken place previously, the fourth part being held by the King.

The Alum Workers.

ESTLING in a lovely valley in the most romantic part of Cleveland lies the little town of Guisborough, with the mouldering ruins of its once famous Priory. At the time of the Conquest it consisted of three manors, which were given to the Earl of Moreton, and soon after, united into one manor, passed to Robert de Brus, Lord of Skelton, to hold *in capite*, by military service. In the year 1129 he founded the Priory for Canons of the Augustine order, and endowed it with a manor of twenty caracutes and two oxgangs, with the tenements, mill, and all other appurtenances. It flourished apace, grew rich, and nurtured some learned and eminent men within its cloisters, until it fell beneath the ruthless axe of Henry VIII.

The Chaloners of Guisborough are of Welsh descent, tracing their ancestry to Trayhayrne, son of Maloc Krwm, one of the fifteen peers of

Wales. His grandson, Madoc, otherwise Chaloner, was ancestor of Thomas Chaloner, of Beaumaris, one of whose sons was Roger Chaloner, a citizen and silk mercer of London, whose son, Sir Thomas, Knight (born 1521), was eminent as a statesman, diplomatist, and poet; was employed on several embassies; was knighted at the battle of Pinkie for bravery; and was author of several esteemed works—"The Praise of Folly," "De Republica Anglorum," and many others. He purchased the manor of Guisborough of Sir Thomas Legh, to whom it had been granted at the Dissolution, for the sum of £998 13s. 4d.

> "These towering rocks, green hills, and spacious plains,
> Circled with wood, are Chaloner's domains.
> A generous race, from Cambro-Griffin traced,
> Fam'd for fair maids and matrons wise and chaste."

His portrait was painted by Holbein and by Antonio More, the former engraved by Holler, the latter exhibited at Leeds in 1868.

Sir Thomas, Knight, his son (born 1559, died 1615), succeeded to the Guisborough estates, and was the discoverer of the alum mines. He was twice married, and had issue several children, of whom the eldest—William—was created baronet in 1620, by the title of Sir William Chaloner, Bart., of Guisborough, in the county of York; Rev. Edward, D.D., an eminent polemical writer; and Thomas and James, Parliamentarian officers and regicides. At college he gained some reputation by his Latin and English verses, but was not equal to his father as a poet. He was, however, a good naturalist, at the time when the science was little understood and less studied. In 1580-84, he made *le grand tour*, and spent some time in Italy, where he associated with all the most eminent literary and scientific men of the day.

Being a keen observer of natural objects and phenomena, he had noticed that on a certain part of his Guisborough estate the soil never froze, that it was speckled with divers colours, chiefly yellow and blue, which sparkled in the sunshine, and that the trees and shrubs which grew thereon spread their roots laterally, and penetrated the earth very superficially, and that their leaves were of a peculiar tint of green. When in Rome he paid a visit to the Pope's alum works at Puzzeoli, where he noticed with his quick, observant eye that the earth and trees presented the same remarkable features as those on his

Guisborough estate, and he immediately came to the conclusion that his land was impregnated with alum. He hastened back to England to test his hypothesis, which he soon verified by experiment, and saw that a mine of wealth lay beneath his feet. But how to work and prepare it he knew not, and there was no one in England who did, and scarcely any one in Europe, outside of Italy, which then had a monopoly of alum, and he set his wits to work to devise some means for separating it from the earth, and preparing it as a manufactured commodity for the market.

Alum is a mineral salt found in clay and other earths, and is a valuable commodity used in various manufactures, and for other purposes. It was first extracted from the earth in which it was embedded, and prepared for use in the East, chiefly at Edessa, in Syria; afterwards near Constantinople; and, on the fall of the Eastern Empire, the alum workers transferred the industry to Italy where it was established in various places, and was confined to the Peninsula for more than a century, after which it spread into Germany, France, and Flanders. The Popes had works at Rome and Civita Vecchia, and carefully guarded their secret, not allowing the workmen to leave the country on any pretence whatever, under pain of excommunication, as the profits of the sale brought a handsome revenue to their coffers.

Sir Thomas Chaloner cogitated the matter in his mind, and the more he thought, the more he saw that the only mode of bringing his alum mines into operation was by kidnapping some of the Pope's workmen, a difficult and perilous task, but which he resolved to attempt, and with that view went again to Italy. Of course the best place for accomplishing his object was at Civita Vecchia, a seaport in the Papal States. Thither, therefore, he went, and lived in retirement, eluding observation as far as possible, but mingling, whenever he could, with the alum workers, ingratiating himself with them by means of wine, friendly and familiar converse, and the judicious distribution of money. By these means he became acquainted with their characters, and with their hopes and aspirations. Three of the more intelligent he singled out to work upon, but each one separately. He would take them into a wine-house and ply them well with the tongue-loosener, and then turn the conversation upon their occupation and future prospects. Of the three, one seemed to have some influence over the other two, who, to a certain extent, took their opinions from him, and re-echoed his sentiments; and Sir Thomas shrewdly perceived that if he could win over this one, the others would follow, like sheep after the bell-wether. They were seated in a wine shop one day, talking over the alum workers' great grievance. "And so," said Sir Thomas, "you would really like to escape from this life of slavery?" "I should, indeed," was the reply; "work here is neither better nor worse than that of a galley-slave." "Why not escape, then, and fling off the chains that gall you?" "Alas, sir," he replied, "we are too closely guarded and watched to render escape at all hopeful. Besides, money would be required, and of this we have but sufficient to get our daily bread." "But if anyone were to put the means of escape in your hands, would you be sufficiently daring to make the attempt?" "Most certainly." "And you would not fear the Pope's excommunication, which would assuredly follow?" "Look here, signor, although I am a poor ignorant alum worker, I know something of what has been doing in England and Germany, and have heard of

Wickcliffe, Luther, and Calvin, and I should care no more for excommunication at the hands of the Pope than I should for a snap of his fingers."

Chaloner saw he had got hold of the right man, and he gradually revealed to him his discovery of alum earth in England, and proposed that he should accompany him thither to work it, where he would be absolutely free, and promising him a much higher remuneration than he was receiving in Italy; to which the man readily assented, and undertook to gain over the other two men, who he felt assured would accompany him. At a subsequent meeting of the four confederates the question was discussed as to the best mode of smuggling them out of Italy, and, after several projects had been suggested and dismissed as impracticable, it was decided that they should be conveyed on board a vessel in casks, as merchandise, and liberated when out at sea.

Sir Thomas at once set to work to find means for carrying out his project, the first being to find a vessel captained by one equally resolute with himself, and to whom he could venture to entrust his secret. Fortunately for his purpose, there chanced to be lying in the harbour a ship from the port of Hull, commanded by an honest fellow-Yorkshireman, a man who, as he said himself, "feared neither the Pope nor the Devil." With this captain he sought an interview, explained who he was, and by careful steps laid his scheme before him. The rough, weather-beaten old captain grasped him by the hand, and, giving it a vigorous shake, swore to stand by him "through thick and thin." He was waiting for a return cargo, had got his vessel half filled, and he agreed, whether full or not, to set sail on that day week. Sir Thomas then went into the market and purchased a quantity of grain, to be delivered on board in six days, packed in casks. He then caused three casks to be constructed secretly, with false ends to be filled with grain, leaving the central part open and pierced with holes, in great number, but so small as to be scarcely perceptible. On the sixth day, when the alum works were closed, the three men came to him, and were placed in the three casks, which, having passed the ordeal of the Customs Office without suspicion, were shipped, and at day-break the following morning the vessel was loosed from her moorings, spread her canvas, and

bade adieu to Civita Vecchia. It was soon discovered at the alum works that the three were
missing, and strict search was made for them,
without result. At length it occurred to the
authorities that they had escaped in the English
vessel which had sailed that morning, and three
ships were sent in pursuit of her, but she had
several hours' start, and had a fair wind, and the
pursuers never caught sight of her. The men
were released from their uncomfortable berths
when at a safe distance, and revelled in their
feeling of liberty as they sped over the blue
waves of the Mediterranean, across the Bay of
Biscay, and up the Channel, arriving safely at
Hull, whence they proceeded with Sir Thomas to
Cleveland.

Sir Thomas established his works beyond
Bellemondegate, where now mountains of refuse
shale are piled up. For some time the works
yielded but small profit, and it was not until
Chaloner got more workmen from Rochelle that
they became a success, after which they yielded a
handsome revenue, and had the effect of breaking
down the Italian monopoly, and reducing the
price of alum in England to one-half its former
cost.

When Chaloner had got the mines and works into thorough working order, King Charles I., at the instigation of some of his rapacious courtiers, made a claim to them as Crown property, and he was compelled to surrender them. They were then let to Sir Paul Pindar, at a rent of £12,500 per annum, to be paid into the Royal Exchequer, besides £1,600 per annum to the Earl of Mulgrave and £600 per annum to Sir William Pennyman, but they were restored to the Chaloners by the Long Parliament. Eight hundred men were employed on the works, and the alum sold at £26 per ton, which left a large residue of profit. Other mines were discovered in Cleveland, on the estates of the families of Phipps, Pennyman, Fairfax, D'Arcy, and Cholmley, when competition brought down the price, and consequently reduced the profits; and, as some of these were situated nearer the sea-coast, with greater facilities for shipment, the Guisborough mines became less and less profitable, and were eventually abandoned.

This conduct on the part of King Charles caused the Chaloners to become zealous Parliamentarians in the Civil War. Sir Thomas's sons, James and Thomas, drew their swords against the King, and both sat as members of the High Court of Justice for his trial. The former was tried as a regicide after the Restoration, was condemned to death, and drawn on a hurdle to Tyburn for execution, but received a reprieve when the halter was round his neck ; was remitted to the Tower, and died of poison, it was reported, by his own hand, "an invention," says Markham, in his Life of Fairfax, "of the carrion vultures of the Restoration."

The latter, at the Restoration, was included in the list of those excluded from pardon, but saved his life by flight. Winstanley says of him, "He had travelled far in the world, and returned home poysoned with that Jesuitical doctrine of King-killing, which he put in practice, being the great speech-maker against the King, . . . and a great stickler for their new Utopian Commonwealth, but upon His Majestie's return fled, his actions being so bad as would not endure the touchstone."

The Maiden of Marblehead.

NE fine summer's morning, in the year of grace 1742, the little inn of the little town of Marblehead was in a state of great bustle, in anticipation of the visit of some Government officials from Boston to dine there. The landlady, rather vixenish in temper and tongue, was busily occupied in attending to the culinary department, and at intervals scolding a young girl of sixteen, who was scrubbing the floor, and was the maid-of-all-work in the establishment, working from early in the morning till late at night for a small pittance of wages.

Marblehead was a small fishing town or village about sixteen miles from Boston, in New England, consisting of a cluster of log-built and straw-thatched houses, amongst which stood conspicuously forth the little hostelry, in consequence of its sign of King George the Second's head swinging and creaking from a crossbeam over the highway. The inhabitants were almost entirely of Guernsey descent, a brave people, but not so loyal as the sign of their inn would seem to indicate, as after the war of the Revolution there were in the town 600 widows of patriots who had fallen; and, in the war of 1812, 500 Marblehead men were prisoners of war in England. The washing of the floor was not completed when the sound of horses' feet was heard coming along the road, and in a few minutes three gentlemen alighted at the door, gave their horses in charge of an extemporised ostler, and entered the house. The landlady made a profound curtsy to her guests, and at the same time rated her hand-maiden for not having the room ready for the gentlemen. " Don't scold her," said he who appeared to be the chief of the group ; " I dare say the little lassie has done her best, and perhaps we have arrived earlier than we were expected." The girl, who was dressed in homely attire, and without shoes or stockings, turned her head with a silent glance of thanks to the speaker—a glance which he pronounced to himself to be angelic.

The gentleman who thus came upon the scene was a Mr. Charles Henry Frankland, thirty-six

Q

years of age, and slightly bronzed in feature from
his early residence in Bengal, where he was born.
He was the eldest son of the Governor of
Bengal, Henry Frankland, who had been
brother and heir-presumptive of Sir Thomas
Frankland, third baronet of Thirkleby, in Yorkshire, but he had died in 1736, leaving this son
heir-presumptive to the baronetcy in his place.
In 1741 he had been appointed Collector of the
Customs at the port of Boston, and on this
summer's morning, with two subordinates was
paying a professional visit to Marblehead, which
lay within the Boston collection. The more he
saw of the girl, as she waited at table during
dinner, the more was he struck with the beauty
of her features and the faultless symmetry of her
figure. As was said of her, " Her ringlets were
black and glossy as the raven ; her dark eyes
beamed with light and loveliness, and her voice
was musical and bird-like." He entered into
conversation with her, and found that her name
was Agnes Surriage, and that her parents, of a
humble position in life, dwelt at a neighbouring
village. He was charmed with the modest and
intelligent replies she made to his questions, but
found that she was altogether uneducated, and

had learnt nothing excepting how to perform household work, to sew and knit, and "to go to meeting on Sundays." On leaving, he gave her money to buy herself shoes and stockings ; but on his next visit he found her again bare-legged, and asking her why she had not supplied herself with shoes and stockings, she replied that she had done so, but kept them to go to "meeting" in.

Becoming more and more fascinated with her beauty, he at length asked her parents to allow him to take her to Boston and have her educated, to which they consented, after some hesitation. He caused her to be instructed in reading, writing, drawing, music, dancing, and all the accomplishments of a fine lady ; but although she excelled eventually in sketching, playing, and dancing, and wrote a beautiful hand, she could never master the difficulties of orthography, her spelling to the last being always of an original and curiously eccentric character.

When her education was completed, and she had grown to womanhood, he took her to his home as his mistress, and she bore him a son, who was christened Richard Cromwell. She was, however, looked upon askance by the Quaker circles of Boston, not on account of her lowly birth, but

because of her disreputable connection with her
"protector."   Sir Thomas Frankland, third
baronet, died without male issue, in 1747, and
Charles Henry, his nephew, succeeded as fourth
baronet. Seven years after, he returned to
England, with Agnes and his son, to dispute the
will of the late baronet as to the disposition of
the family estates at Thirkleby, near Easingwold.
Sir Thomas made three wills; the first in 1741,
wherein he left a slender provision for his widow,
leaving the estates to his heir-male.   In the
second, made in 1744, he left Thirkleby to his
widow for life, to pass at her death to the then
holder of the baronetcy; and by the third will,
dated 1746, he left her the estates, producing
£2,500 per annum, and the whole of his person-
alty absolutely, and to dispose of as she chose.
It was contended that the last will was made
when he was in an unsound state of mind and
under undue influence, and a lawsuit ensued,
resulting in the setting aside of the third and the
confirmation of the second will.   The lawsuit
gained, Sir Charles and Agnes went for a tour
on the Continent, and in the month of November, 1755, were sojourning in the city of Lisbon.
On the 1st of that month, the sun rose, shining

with almost unusual brightness, and the streets
were filled with people going hither and thither
on matters of religion, business, and pleasure,
little dreaming of, and with nothing to indicate,
the catastrophe which was to befall their city.
The Franklands had breakfasted at their hotel,
and Sir Charles, donning a Court suit, started off
in a carriage with a lady to witness the celebration of High Mass in the Cathedral, leaving
Agnes at the hotel. They had not proceeded
far, and were passing in front of a lofty building,
when, without warning, the terrible earthquake
occurred, which in eight minutes laid the city in
ruins, and swallowed up 50,000 of its inhabitants.
The lofty building came crashing down, and
buried the carriage and its occupants. What
became of the lady is not known, but the horses
were killed, and Sir Charles lay bruised and
wounded beneath the ruins for an hour. In full
expectation of death, he reflected on his past life,
and, concluding that he was undergoing a judgment of God for his misdeeds, and especially for
having lived in a state of concubinage, made a vow
that if he should be rescued, he would show his
repentance by marrying the partner of his guilt.
Agnes had escaped unhurt, and when the first

shock had passed, fearful that some mischance
had befallen him, rushed out in the direction of
the cathedral, regardless of the still falling
houses, in search of him. As she was clambering
over a heap of ruins, she heard moans issuing
from beneath, and a voice which she recognised
as that of her beloved one. She immediately
got together a party of diggers, and, by promises
of high rewards, succeeded in extricating him,
and after his wounds had been dressed, conveyed
him to Belem, where, in process of time, he
recovered, and where their marriage was celebrated.

Sir Charles returned to Boston; but in 1757
he was appointed Consul-General to Portugal,
and again came to Lisbon. In 1763 he resumed
his duties at Boston, retaining his consulship,
although absent, until 1767, when he returned to
England, and died the following year, being
succeeded in the baronetcy by his brother
Thomas.

Lady Frankland returned to New England
with her son, and they resided upon an estate at
Hopkinson which she had inherited through her
parents, but at the outbreak of the Revolu-
tionary war in 1775, she, being a Royalist, came

to England, and, in 1782, married Mr. John Drew, a banker at Chichester, and died in 1783.

Richard Cromwell, her son, entered the naval service of England, but retired on his ship being ordered to America, as he felt unwilling to fight against his native land. In 1796 he was living in Chichester with a family growing up around him.

In 1865 there was published at Albany, "Sir Charles Henry Frankland, Bart.; or, Boston in the Colonial Times; by Elias Nason, M.A.," who, in the preface, says—"Who was Sir C. H. Frankland? is a question which a brief story entitled 'A legend of New England,' and published by William Lincoln, in 1843, and still more recently the ballad of 'Agnes,' by Dr. Oliver Wendell Holmes here, led the public to entertain: Was he a real person or a myth? Was there ever such a collector of the port of Boston? Was he indeed buried under the ruins of Lisbon at the time of the great earthquake? Was he rescued therefrom by the efforts of a poor girl, named Agnes Surriage, and did he afterwards make her his wife?" These questions the author answers in the subsequent pages of the pamphlet, of which the above is an epitome.

Rise of the House of Phipps.

ABOUT the middle of the seventeenth century, during the Civil War and the Restoration, there dwelt in Bristol one James Phipps, a gunsmith by trade. He was blessed with a numerous progeny; of him it might truly be said that "his quiver was full of them," for he had eventually twenty-six children, of whom twenty-one were boys. Having only his gunmaking trade to depend upon for a living, he found it difficult to provide means for feeding, clothing, and educating them, and often lay awake long at nights, pondering in his mind what he should do to meet the necessities of the case. At that time, and for two or three reigns previously, we had been at work laying the foundations of the present great American Republic, by establishing plantations of colonists, aristocratic and Episcopalian, in the south, and Puritanical in the north, most of whom had been driven thither by the persecutions they had undergone in the mother country. Bristol was then the great port of imports and exports of the Western Continent, and James Phipps naturally heard of the unbounded capabilities of the new continent, as also he heard, by tradition, of the vast wealth which the buccaneers of Elizabeth's reign—the old Vikings of Devonshire—brought from the West Indies, Peru, Mexico, etc., into the ports of Bristol, Barnstaple, Bideford, etc., and it occurred to him that here was scope enough for him and all his sons, and he emigrated with them to New England, where William, his youngest son, was born, and he seems to have died soon after, as this son is stated to have been brought up by his mother until he was eighteen years of age.

This William Phipps was the founder of that family who are now lords of Mulgrave Castle, and whose dignity has culminated in a Marquisate. He had received no education, but taught himself to read and write when apprentice to a ship carpenter. At the expiration of his apprenticeship he married the daughter of Captain Robert Spencer, and relict of a rich merchant of the name of Hull, who brought him a small fortune, with which he

commenced business, but his speculations were
not successful.   But he did not despair, although
fortune did seem to frown.   He was a man
of unbounded enterprise and energy, and he said
to his wife, who was lamenting the loss of her
money, " Be not cast down, my dear ; I will live
to be the commander of better men than I myself
am now.   Providence has great things in store for
me, and the time shall come when I will build a
fair brick house in the green lane of North
Boston, of which you shall be the mistress."
When casting about for employment, he chanced
to hear of a Spanish galleon, laden with specie
and plate, which had been wrecked half a century
previously somewhere in the Bahamas, and he
resolved to go in search of it, and to endeavour
the recovery of the cargo by means of the diving-
bell.

Aristotle, 300 years B.C., makes some obscure
references to a machine of this kind, but what it
was or how employed is not known.   The first
reliable account we have of such a machine
is given by Taisnier, who describes a "cacobus
aquaticus" (marine kettle) which was exhibited
by two Greeks before the Emperor Charles V.,
at Toledo, in 1538 ; but it seems to have been of

no practical use, as it had no apparatus for supplying the divers with fresh air. A similar sort of bell, but constructed on better principles, had been made use of on the coast of Mull, between the years 1650 and 1660 to operate upon some sunken vessels of the Spanish Armada, but without much success. It was this which directed the attention of Phipps to the diving-bell, who perceived that by various modifications and improvements of the apparatus it might be made a most valuable instrument for submarine operations, and after a long and patient study, and numberless experiments, he succeeded in constructing a bell very much the same as that now used, and capable of being worked much more efficiently and with greater safety than any previously employed. In consequence of his having thus, by his skill and scientific modifications, produced a really working machine, he is generally styled " the inventor of the diving-bell." He sailed for the Bahamas, but was not able to find the spot where the vessel lay. He received information of another, however, the position of which was more accurately defined, and which held a much greater treasure.

He then sailed for London, his resources having

failed, where he arrived in 1683, and laid the project before King Charles, who furnished him with a 19-gun frigate, in which he returned to the Bahamas. Before he found the locality of the object of his search, he again became crippled for funds, and went again to London for further assistance, but King James, who had succeeded to the crown in the interval, deeming his views visionary, declined having anything to do in the matter. The Duke of Albemarle, however, was more sanguine and got up a subscription for a fresh outfit, on condition that he and the subscribers should share in the proceeds, and Captain Phipps sailed with two vessels. This time he was more successful ; after some search he found the precise spot where the galleon lay, and, by means of his diving-bell, brought up from the wreck thirty-two tons of silver, besides gold plate and jewels, of the estimated value of £200,000. With this splendid prize he came again to England, but on a division of the spoil, he got no more than £20,000, the Duke absorbing £90,000, whilst the remainder was distributed amongst the other subscribers and the crews of the vessels. The King, in appreciation of his ingenuity and enterprise, knighted him, and constituted him Sheriff of New England. He made a second visit to the wreck, and made a gleaning of what had been left, and on his return to New England he built the "fair brick house in the green lane of North Boston," where he dwelt some time with his wife, now Lady Phipps, who no longer twitted him about the loss of her fortune. He afterwards served in the army, and was appointed, by William III., Governor of Massachusetts; but two years after, refusing to sanction certain corrupt practices, he was charged by his enemies with maladministration of his government. He went to London to clear himself of the false charges, but died there soon after his arrival, in 1694, and was buried in the Church of St. Mary Woolnoth, London, where his widow erected a sumptuous monument to his memory, with a sculptured representation of his achievements in the Bahamas.

Not having any issue by his wife, he adopted Constantine, her nephew, and at his death bequeathed to him the bulk of his fortune. He is said generally, in the genealogies of the family, to have been Phipps's own son; but in "The Life of his Excellency Sir William Phipps, Kt., late Captain-General and Governor-in-Chief of

.the Province of Massachusetts Bay, New England, 1697," which was published during the lifetime of his widow, it is said distinctly, "not having any child of his own, he adopted a nephew of his wife to be his heir." Sir Constantine Phipps, his nephew, who assumed the name of Phipps on inheriting his uncle's property, became Lord High Chancellor of Ireland, was 'knighted, and died in 1728. William, his son, married the Lady Katherine, daughter of James, fourth Earl of Anglesey, by the Lady Katherine Darnley, a natural daughter of King James II., who re-married John Sheffield, Duke of Buckingham, Duke and Marquis of Normandy, and Earl of Mulgrave. Constantine, his son, who died 1780, was created Baron Mulgrave of New Ross, in the Peerage of Ireland, in 1768. Constantine, his son, second Baron, was the famous navigator, who made a voyage of discovery into the Arctic regions, and was, in the Pitt Administration, Joint Paymaster of the Forces, a Lord of Trade, and a Commissioner of the India Board. He was created, in 1790, Baron Mulgrave, of Mulgrave Castle, in the Peerage of England, but, dying issueless in 1792, that title expired. His portrait may be seen in Greenwich Hospital.

Henry, his brother, succeeded as third Baron Mulgrave of New Ross, and in his person the Barony of Mulgrave, of Mulgrave Castle, was re-created in 1794. He was further created Viscount Normanby and Earl of Mulgrave, in 1812, and G.C.B. He was Governor of Scarborough Castle and Foreign Secretary, 1805-6, and died in 1831. Constantine Henry, his son, succeeded to all his father's titles, and was advanced in the Peerage to the Marquisate of Normanby, in 1838. His Lordship, who died in 1863, was an eminent statesman and diplomatist, was constituted P.C., 1832; G.C.H., 1832; G.C.B., 1847; and K.G., 1851, and held the following offices:—Governor-General of Jamaica, 1832-34; Lord Privy Seal, July to November, 1834; Lord-Lieutenant of Ireland, 1835-39; Secretary of State for the Colonies, September to December, 1839; Home Secretary, 1839-41; was Minister at Paris, 1846-52; Envoy Extraordinary and Minister Plenipotentiary at Florence, 1854-58; and represented Scarborough in Parliament, 1818-20, Higham Ferrers, 1822-26, and Malton, 1826-30. He was a man of accomplished literary

taste, having published " A Year of Revolution,"
from a journal kept in Paris, in the year 1848,
2 vols., 1857. Also several novels—" Yes and
No," " Matilda," " The Contrast," " Clorinde,"
and " The Prophet of St. Paul's," and several
political pamphlets of great ability, with some
other minor works. George Augustus Constantine, his son, the second Marquis was a K.C.MG.
and P.C. ; was M.P. for Scarborough, 1847-21 ;
Treasurer of the Household, 1853-58 ; a Lord-in-
Waiting in 1866 and 1868-69 ; Captain of the
Corps of Gentlemen-at-Arms, 1869-71 ; Governor of Nova Scotia, 1858-66 ; of Queensland,
1871-74 ; of New Zealand, 1874-78 ; and of
Victoria, 1878-84. He died in 1890, and was
succeeded by his son, the Rev. Constantine
Charles Henry, the present Marquis, who was
born in 1846.

The Traitor Governor of Hull.

OCTOBER the thirtieth, 1640, was a day of great bustle and excitement in the town of Beverley. All ordinary business seemed to be suspended, and the streets were filled with groups of people, 'in earnest discussion, and with persons hastening hither and thither as if on important business, whilst great crowds of burghers occupied the space in front of the old Hanse House or Guildhall, waiting for the opening of the doors. It was the day appointed for the election of representatives to Parliament, and as such an event had not taken place since 1628, excepting that of the spring of the present year, for the Parliament which lasted only twenty-eight days, combined with the irritating circumstances which had caused the issue of the writs, the excitement and the depth of party feeling between the Puritans and the upholders of the policy of Wentworth and Laud, was all the more intense. The King had striven

R

to rule and levy taxes absolutely and irresponsibly, contrary to the Constitution ; and the murmurs and opposition became so great as to compel him to summon together the representatives of the Commons to sanction his acts, and grant the necessary subsidies.   Hence were the burgesses of Beverley summoned together to elect their representatives to what came to be called in after time " The Long Parliament."   In due course they were admitted into the hall, and presently after the Mayor, William Cheppelow, a mercer, entered, and took his seat as Returning-Officer. He was accompanied by the Recorder, Francis Thorpe, the Aldermen, the Capital Burgesses, and the usual officials.   After the reading of the writ and other preliminaries, he asked if any one had a candidate to propose, when a burgess proposed Sir John Hotham, " our old representative, who has served us faithfully in four previous Parliaments."   Another proposed Michael Warton, Esq., " our worthy townsman, whose principles are well known to us all ; " and a third proposed Sir Thomas Metham, Knight, all which proposals were seconded, and the polling proceeded with, the result being the return of the two former, who, the following day, posted up to London to take their seats at the opening of the House on the third of November.

Sir John Hotham was a descendant of Sir John de Trehouse, Knight, of Kilkenny, who, for his services at the Battle of Hastings, had a grant of the Manor of Hotham, near Beverley. Peter, his great-grandson, assumed the name of "de Hotham," and his descendant, Sir John, was summoned as Baron in 1315, which dignity became extinct at his death, as it was a personal summons only. The family subsequently became possessors of South Dalton and Scorborough, both in the neighbourhood of Beverley, which were now held by Sir John, who made the mansion at the latter village his place of residence. He was born towards the end of the sixteenth century, was made a baronet in 1621, and had been five times married. He was now destined, by reason of his return to the Long Parliament, to make his name famous in English history, or, as some might say, infamous. He was not disaffected towards the King and his policy; what he did in opposition thereto he deemed to be his duty to the Parliament of which he was a member, of which, however, he afterwards repented, impelled partly also by jealousy at the appointment of Lord Fairfax to the command of the forces in the north, which, he considered, ought to have been given to him, an old experienced soldier, who had served for a long time in the Low Countries, and had fought under the banner of the Elector Palatine at the Battle of Prague.

At the neighbouring town of Hull there was at this time a great store of arms and ammunition, which had been deposited there for the use of the troops in the Scottish expedition, when the King went thither to attempt to cram the Liturgy down the throats of the Presbyterian Scots. It had been under the charge of Colonel Legge, who, on the disbandment of the army, left it under the care of the Mayor of Hull. When the rupture between the King and the Parliament was coming to a crisis, the former went with his Court to York, his secret object being to get possession of the magazine; and the Parliament, suspecting his motive for going north, sent Sir John Hotham and his son, Captain John Hotham, to take charge of it, and not to deliver it up on any consideration, excepting by their order. This occurred in March, 1642. Captain Hotham, his

son, represented Scarborough in the Long
Parliament.

In March, the King had sent the Earl of
Newcastle to take charge of Hull and the
magazine of arms, but the Mayor declined
delivering up his trust, and the following month
the King proceeded thither in person, to demand
admittance, attended by a suite of noblemen and
gentlemen. When he appeared before the town,
he found the gates shut, the drawbridges raised,
and the walls swarming with men-at-arms. He
caused a trumpet to be sounded for a parley,
when Sir John Hotham, the new governor,
accompanied by the Mayor, appeared over
Beverley Gate. He had previously sent Sir Louis
Dives from Beverley with a message that he was
coming with some noblemen to dine with Sir
John, who held a hurried consultation with
Alderman Pelham, a Member of the Parliament,
when they determined upon not admitting him,
and upon placing a guard over the Mayor and
burgesses, and sent a reply that he could not
admit him without a betrayal of the trust
reposed in him by the Parliament. When Sir
John appeared over the gate, the King
demanded admittance, and asked angrily why the

gate was shut against him. Sir John replied, " I am sorry to disobey your Majesty, but I am intrusted by the Parliament with the charge of this garrison, with instructions to admit no one who comes with apparently hostile intentions, and I trust that I may not be misunderstood, for nothing is meant in it but the good of the kingdom and the welfare of your Majesty." "Pray, Sir John, by what authority do you act thus disloyally?" "By order of both Houses of Parliament." "Read or show me that authority." "I decline doing so." "Has the Mayor seen it?" "No! I scorn that he should. I am the Governor of the town, and it concerns no one else."

The King then asked the Mayor if he sanctioned this treasonable conduct, who, terrified and abashed in the presence of Royalty, fell on his knees and replied, " My liege! glad should I be to open the gates if it were in my power; but, alas! both I and the inhabitants are under guard, and soldiers, with drawn swords, threaten our lives if we make the attempt."

" Well, Sir John," said the King, " this act of yours is unparalleled, and will, I fear, lead to dismal consequences, and I cannot do less than

proclaim and proceed against you as a traitor;
but I will give you an hour to decide." He then
retired, and, on his return, found the Governor in-
flexible in his refusal to admit him, excepting
with a following of not more than twenty persons,
upon which he caused a herald to proclaim him
a traitor, and all who abetted him guilty of
treason, shouting, "Fling the traitor over the
walls! Throw the rebel into the ditch," after
which he retired to Beverley, and spent the night
there. The following morning he sent a
messenger with a promise of pardon for the past,
and his favour for the future, if Sir John would
open the gates to him, and when he received a
negative answer he returned to York. The
King then sent a complaint to Parliament of Sir
John's conduct, who replied that he had done
quite right, and that his proclamation of him as a
traitor was a flagrant breach of the privilege of
Parliament.

As the King could not obtain admission to the
town by persuasive means, he resorted to force,
and laid siege to it, and the Parliament sent an
additional force of 2,000 men to maintain the defence. About this time, Lord Digby, a Royalist,
was captured and brought into Hull, who, in

repeated conversations with Sir John on the evils he was bringing upon the kingdom, half persuaded him to admit the King; but eventually he resolved not to betray his trust. Nevertheless he facilitated the escape of his lordship, and this was what first caused him to be viewed with suspicion by the Parliament. Soon after, the King went into the Midlands, and set up his standard at Nottingham, leaving the siege of Hull in the hands of Lord Newport, and the civil war commenced in earnest. Captain Hotham, a dashing and dare-devil officer, left Hull with a small force, had a brush with and was defeated by Glemham, on the Wolds; frightened Archbishop Williams from Cawood, who fled to Wales, and never saw his diocese again; disputed the passage of the Tees with Newcastle, and again at Tadcaster against an overwhelming force; and assisted Sir T. Fairfax in the capture of Leeds.

By various instrumentalities, the Hothams, father and son, had now veered round from the Parliamentarian to the Royalist side. The younger had met the Queen when she landed at Burlington, kissed her hand, and promised obedience to the King's will; and the elder had been

in correspondence with Newcastle, and had under-
taken to deliver up Hull on the 28th of August.
But all this had come to the ears of
Parliament, and measures were at once taken to
frustrate his intentions. Orders were sent to
Thomas Raikes, the Mayor, Sir Matthew Boynton,
Hotham's brother-in-law, and Captain Meyer,
commander of a vessel of war in the Humber, to
arrest him and his son, and send them up to
London, and they lost no time in the matter.
Captain Meyer landed one hundred men, who
seized the citadel and the block-house, and they
placed a watch round Sir John's house. Captain
Hotham they captured without difficulty, and
placed in security during the night, and at
daylight went to Sir John's house to take
him, but found he had effected his escape.

Too old a soldier to be caught in a trap like
that, and too old in strategy not to be able to devise means of extrication from a peril, he,
having learned from his spies what was passing,
and seeing that matters were coming to a crisis,
determined upon flying to his house at
Scorborough, which was fortified and able to
stand a short siege. He eluded the watch by
passing out by a private door at the back, and

made his way, by obscure lanes and streets, to Beverley Gate. When he arrived there he was saluted by the guard, who knew nothing of the order for his arrest, and, assuming a lofty unembarrassed bearing, he ordered the gate to be opened and six of the guards to follow him to Beverley. He was immediately obeyed, and, securing a horse, he rode off in the direction of Beverley ; but as soon as he had purposely outridden his attendants, he turned to the right, through Sculcoates, towards Stone Ferry. His pursuers meanwhile learnt what had passed at the gate, and rode after him along the Beverley road. They overtook the six guards, who informed them that Sir John could not be more than a few furlongs ahead on the road, and they spurred on towards Beverley without overtaking the fugitive.

Sir John's house lay three or four miles beyond Beverley, on the west of the river Hull, and as he knew it would be dangerous to pass through the town, he resolved to cross the river and proceed along the eastern side, and re-cross it when he had passed Beverley. Unfortunately, when he came to Stone Ferry, there was no boat, and the river was running too rapidly to allow

of swimming his horse across; he therefore
hastened on to Wawn Ferry, hoping to cross
there, but the fates seemed to be against him;
there was no boat there either, and the hazard
was too great to attempt reaching the opposite
bank by any other means. He paused for a few
minutes, thinking over what course he should
pursue. There appeared to be nothing for it but
to make a bold dash through Beverley. It was
true that the town was held by the Parliamentarians, but they might not have heard of the
events which had transpired in Hull. Besides,
there was no alternative, and putting spurs to his
horse's flanks, he soon came in sight of the towers
of Beverley Minster. He entered the town by
Queensgate, and passing along the streets with
an air of indifference, came to the Market-place,
which he found occupied by a troop of 700 or 800
men, with his nephew, Colonel Boynton, at their
head. With an assumed nonchalant air, he
saluted his nephew, and ordered a company of the
men to follow, which they were preparing to do,
when the Colonel, who had been made acquainted
with his treachery, came up, and seizing his
horse's bridle, said, "Sir John, you are my
prisoner. I respect you as my kinsman, but I

must, although with the greatest reluctance, pass by all tender respect, and arrest you as a traitor to the Commonwealth." Sir John, seeing that resistance was useless, replied, " Well, kinsman, since such is your will I must be content and submit," but, espying a lane close by, he clapped spurs to his horse and galloped down it, followed by his nephew, shouting " Down with the traitor; knock him down;" and a soldier, striking him with the butt end of his musket, brought him to the earth, bleeding and almost senseless. By a strange coincidence, he was confined for the night in the same house where the King had slept after his discomfiture at the gates of Hull. The following morning he was taken to Hull, placed on board Captain Meyer's vessel, and, with his son, immediately conveyed to London. On the 3rd of December they were arraigned at the Guildhall for treason, the Earl of Manchester presiding, and were sentenced to be executed on the last day of the year. The House of Lords, desirous of pardoning him, reprieved Sir John for three days; but the Commons would not listen to it. Captain Hotham was beheaded in due course before his father, which some said was a piece of concerted malice, that he might not die a baronet, which he would have done had his father suffered first.

On the 2nd of January, Sir John was brought out upon Tower Hill and mounted the scaffold, accompanied by the Rev. Hugh Peters and other ministers and friends. He met his fate bravely and like a soldier, and before laying his head on the block, addressed the people, saying—"Gentlemen,—I know no more of myself but that I deserve this death from God Almighty, and that I deserve damnation and the severest punishment from Him. As for the business of Hull—the betraying it from the Parliament—the ministers that have all been with me and gave me good counsels, I thank them. Neither was I any ways guilty of it. That's all I can say to that act," etc., etc.

It will be seen that he was no orator, and did not give utterance to his ideas in a very clear and coherent manner. The speech of his son, three days previously, was very superior, both in matter and manner.

After Peters had addressed the crowd, putting Sir John's sentiments in better language, the unfortunate baronet placed his

head on the block.   His head was stricken
off by the headsman, and his mutilated
remains were buried in the church of All-
Hallows, Barking, the liturgy being read at his
funeral, although it had been abolished by Act
of Parliament.

Elegantly bound in cloth gilt, demy 8vo., price, 6s.

𝔜𝔬𝔯𝔨𝔰𝔥𝔦𝔯𝔢 𝔅𝔞𝔱𝔱𝔩𝔢𝔰.

By EDWARD LAMPLOUGH.

CONTENTS:

THIS work contains carefully-written accounts of the following Yorkshire Battles, which cannot fail to interest and instruct the reader. It is a book of more than local interest :—

Opinions of the Press.

*LONDON: SIMPKIN, MARSHALL, HAMILTON, KENT, & CO.
HULL: WILLIAM ANDREWS & CO., THE HULL PRESS.*

Old=Time Punishments.

By WILLIAM ANDREWS, F.R.H.S.,

AUTHOR OF "CURIOSITIES OF THE CHURCH," "HISTORIC ROMANCE,"
"FAMOUS FROSTS AND FROST FAIRS," "HISTORIC
YORKSHIRE," ETC.

CONTENTS.

Carefully prepared papers, profusely illustrated, appear
on the following subjects :—

*The Ducking Stool—The Brank, or Scold's Bridle—The Pillory—
Punishing Authors and burning books—Finger-Pillory—The Jougs
—The Stocks—The Drunkard's Cloak—Whipping—Public Penance
in White Sheets—The Repentance-Stool—Riding the Stang—Gibbet
Lore—Drowning—Burning to Death—Boiling to Death—Beheading
—Hanging, Drawing, and Quartering—Pressing to Death—
Hanging—Hanging in Chains—The Halifax Gibbet—The Scottish
Maiden, etc.—An Index of five closely-printed pages.*

MANY CURIOUS ILLUSTRATIONS.

PRESS OPINIONS.

"This is an entertaining book . . . well-chosen illustrations and a serviceable
index."—*Athenæum.*
" A hearty reception may be bespoken for it."—*Globe.*
" A work which will be eagerly read by all who take it up."—*Scotsman.*
" It is entertaining."—*Manchester Guardian.*
" A vast amount of curious and entertaining matter."—*Sheffield Independent.*
" We can honestly recommend a perusal of this book."—*Yorkshire Post.*
" Interesting, and handsomely printed."—*Newcastle Chronicle.*
" A very readable history."—*Birmingham Daily Gazette.*
"Mr. Andrews' book is well worthy of careful study, and is a perfect mine of
wealth on the subject of which it treats."—*Herts Advertiser.*
" It is sure of a warm welcome on both sides of the Atlantic."—*Christian Leader.*

LONDON : SIMPKIN, MARSHALL, HAMILTON, KENT, & CO.
HULL : WILLIAM ANDREWS & CO., THE HULL PRESS.

www.ingramcontent.com/pod-product-compliance
Lightning Source LLC
Chambersburg PA
CBHW031346020726
47499CB00005B/1419